THE STORMER

By

Gurmeet Mattu

For Leanne

Davina was her name and she pleaded that I should not write this, that I should not expose her to the world. Apologies, sweet Davey, whose standard would I bear if your starlit eyes had not so pleaded. Those days are gone.

1. THE WALL AND THE PEOPLE

See wee Hugh, way up there, high in the sky, splashing on paint like there was a world glut - a paint lake? A paint mountain?

There's a heap of red, because he's on her hair now, and he's got to get it right, tints of yellow, splashes of orange.

And her? She's washing dishes, of course, like she always does.

Up in the cool fresh air, the sun blazing down, Hugh wiped the sweat from his forehead. Nudes always did that to him.

Took a breather, leaning on the scaffolding, looked out over the city. This wee guy, barely five five, with his shaggy hair and moustache, unkempt, unloved, this heartbreaker.

Oh Glasgow.

See, there were these three kids once, grew up together in that fair city, nation of Scotland, continent of Europe.

They went to school together, played together, fought together.

They knew each other well, and in the way of such things they became lovers and haters, winners and losers, dreamers and the dreamed about.

Their names were Hugh Cooper, the hero of our tale; Crawford Gillespie, the villain; and Davina McLean, the Stormer.

Later, Crawford became a policeman, the crown prince of the Strathclyde Force, and married the beautiful Davina.

And Hugh? Well, Hugh's way up there, high in the sky, splashing paint all over Glasgow.

It's what he does, creates his art, hanging outside a renovated tenement building, its stone-work sand-blasted to the colour of cream. At its side is a vacant lot, a piece of waste ground, now being landscaped by workmen. They are creating a little city garden with patches of grass, flower beds, a rockery, park benches. It's nice.

3

There is scaffolding across the gable end, and much of it is shrouded in canvas. But there's a gap in the canvas, high up on the wall, because Hugh needs light to work.

He is ladling on the paint with a large brush, like any other busy artisan. The paint he is enthusiastically throwing onto the wall is an orangey red.

A very similar orangey red to the overalls Fiona was wearing. Fiona was a smallish and feisty-looking blonde in her mid 20s, with a cuddly look that was deceptive.

She walked towards a cubicle, carrying a pile of towels. The massage parlour was pine-panelled and hygienic looking, though a little faded. Fiona entered the cubicle where a fat, naked, man was lying face down on the couch. Fiona dumped the towels, poured oil on the man's back and began massaging.

After a while his hand dropped from his side, to brush against her leg. Getting braver, he stroked her leg. Fiona sighed resignedly, took a pencil from her pocket and moved it towards the man's backside where she made one rapid stabbing motion. There was a sharp intake of breath, and his hand withdrew quickly from her leg. Fiona returned the to pencil to her pocket and, having dealt with the occupational hazard, returned to taking care of the fat man's less carnal needs.

Meanwhile, Hugh climbed down the ladder, watched by two 10 year old boys. The boys had been annoying the gardeners, but those of the green fingers had finished for the day and were packing their van. Hugh got to the bottom and started fussing about with paint cans, mixing up a new batch of paint. The two boys came over to watch what he was doing, then looked up at the wall.

Finally the smaller boy gathered his courage and asked the question with a cough. "What is it, mister ?"

His friend, the sophisticate, answered for Hugh. "It's a muriel, ya wanker."

The younger lad, a budding art critic, was all eagerness. "Is it? Let's see it, mister, go on."

Hugh dealt with them as he had been dealt with when young. "Bugger off."

He continued stirring the paint, the same orangey-red.

Very similar in colour to the red hair of Davina.
She was washing dishes.
Plate.   Into the basin of soapy water.   Good scrub.   Rinse under running tap.   Stack.
She was one of the few people in the world who had actually been trained to wash dishes. Her mother had been that kind of woman.
Davina was five foot eleven inches tall. Her inside leg was 38 inches, and her legs had good tone and shape.   She took size six shoes. Her bum was small and neat, and yet well defined. Her hips were 34 inches, her waist was 22 inches and her stomach was flat and tight. Her chest was 34 inches, but she had a narrow back and took a C cup. Her skin was flawless, without blemishes, marks or scars.   It was the colour of light honey.   Her hair was the flaming orange of a promising evening, and her face was that dream of symmetry and perfection. Wide eyes, hazy grey.   Retrousse nose.   Wide mouth.   High cheekbones. Dimple in chin.   She had Audrey Hepburn's neck.
She finished the dishes and dried her hands.   There was a pile of housework to do, but she didn't feel like it.   She never did.
Why did semi-detached, three bedroom houses in Bearsden take so much cleaning?   Davina didn't know it, but it was an unavoidable law of nature.   When you moved into the middle class suburbs from a working class tenement, your time and effort expenditure didn't increase in proportion to the increase in living space.   It rose in direct relationship to the value of the new property.   Once I was poor and dirty, now I am rich and clean.
She was wearing a pair of faded denims and a cheesecloth blouse.   Apart from that she was bare-foot, bare-assed, and bare-boobed. The animal lurked inside her yet.
She made a cup of lemon tea, took it through to the lounge and curled up on the leather settee.   Her breathing was slow and settled as she sipped, she was waiting.   Soon, she slept and when she awoke she made the transformation that was expected of her.   She went through to the bedroom and became

a lady, dressing as befitted the wife of a superintendent of police.

Her bedroom was well-appointed, fitting for a nice middle-class couple.

Davina tried on different clothes in front of a full-length mirror. One skirt was a fraction above the knee and obviously pleased her, because she swished about in it. The front door slammed and Crawford, her husband, tall and distinguished in his police superintendent's uniform, appeared at the bedroom door, saw the amount of leg displayed, frowned and shook his head. It was an order.

Hugh was packing up his equipment and soaking his brushes as an old Volvo pulled up and Fiona got out. She kissed Hugh warily, avoiding his painted surfaces, then stood back while he continued packing. When his attention was away from her, she began edging towards the scaffolding. But Hugh noticed her out of the side of his eye. Just as she got to the canvas and made furtive attempts to pull it away, he made a leap towards her. There was a little mock struggle and she ran away from him to the other end of the wall, to hold the other edge of the canvas and threaten to lift it. He stalked towards her and she lifted the canvas a little higher. The threat was implicit, one step further and she would lift the canvas and look. Hugh, stymied, dropped to his knees and threw open his arms, begging her not to. She laughed and came towards him, kissed him this time without caring about the paint. She helped him pack his gear into the boot of the car and they drove away from the tenement wall.

A large dark Audi pulled up outside the church and Crawford got out and opened the passenger door for Davina. She was dressed very demurely in a tweed suit.

They walked towards the church, where other police officers and various, dignified and suited, middle-aged men were gathering. They were all accompanied by wives, all dressed soberly, but not quite as rigidly as Davina. There was much genteel hand-shaking and back slapping, but it was Crawford who participated. Davina was left standing alone and

Crawford had to come back for her to escort her into the church.

The Dog's Breath, a grubby bar which had no character apart from its customers. There were students, an arty crowd, bikers, actors, poets, derelicts, nurses and workmen. It was noisy, a jukebox blaring, and there was heavy drinking going on.

Hugh and Fiona entered the pub and struggled through the crowd towards Midden, leather-jacketed, bearded and long-haired, standing with a crowd of other bikers. Hugh reached the bar and waved over Bob, the manager. He passed him a cheque he produced from an envelope and asked him, in a loud voice, to cash it.

Bob wondered, and knew that Hugh knew, that the days of signing the backs of cheques was long gone, but glancing at the slip, was wise to his purpose. He whistled dutifully. "This is for ten grand, Hugh, I can't cash that."

Hugh gave a gleeful explanation, "Came this morning, wages for the painting from the council. Give me a sub on it."

Bob joined him in his moment of glory, "You'll be buying everybody a drink then?"

Hugh glanced round at the huge number of people in the bar and shrugged, "Damn right."

The service had just ended and the congregation were slowly filing out. There was a lot of chatting between the business types, networking. The police officers had their own little section and as they left Chief Constable Burroughs put his arm round Crawford's shoulder.

"I hate these duty calls," Burroughs said, "Half these buggers are probably laundering some ill-gotten gains."

Crawford nodded. "Yes, but a very thought-provoking sermon, I thought."

Burroughs looked at him quizzically, but then shrugged it off.

"I noticed Stoker was here," Burroughs commented "Shows initiative for a young fellow."

"He'll go far, sir. I'll keep an eye out for him."

"Henderson was late, saw him sneaking in at the end."

Crawford could not help but agree with his superior. "He's slow with his paperwork too. Room there for improvement, if you ask me. But at least he showed up."

Burroughs nodded, not really looking at Crawford.

"Your Davina looked stunning, as usual."

Crawford smiled gratefully, then looked round, puzzled, searching for Davina. Her mane of red hair identified her, sitting alone, eyes closed, half asleep in the near empty church.

Back in the Dog's Breath everybody was drunk to various degrees. Hugh turned to the throng of bikers surrounding him and said, "You're not all turning up, and that's final. It's my big day and I'm not having you screwing it up."

Midden, smiling wickedly, cuddled up to him. "We want to see your picture, Hugh. This masterpiece, that's going to make you world famous ... well, locally speaking."

Hugh shrugged him off. "You can see it after the opening. I'm not having you there noising everybody up and stealing the drink."

Midden was staggered. "Drink? You never said there was drink involved."

Hugh sensed danger and pulled Fiona aside. "You make sure that arsehole brother of yours doesn't turn up."

Fiona comforted him with a smile. "They won't be there, they're only winding you up. They know it's important to you."

Midden came up behind Hugh and thrust his wiry frame against Hugh's butt. "Hugh! Can I shag you when you're famous ?"

The following morning City Council vans and lorries arrived at the tenement. Workmen and equipment poured out of these. Rubbish was cleared from the newly-landscaped waste ground in front of the gable end and carted away in trucks. A little stage was erected at the side with a line of chairs, and a little podium was placed on it with a microphone on a stand. A small marquee was put up beside it. Tables were set up and caterers arrived to lay out a buffet and wine.

Fiona's flat was girlie. Pastel shades and teddy bears. The style was poor, but the expensive looking TV, DVD and surround sound system showed that this was down to a lack of taste, not cash.

Fiona was still running around in her knickers, but Hugh was dressed, wearing the same T-shirt, jeans and long coat he had worn the day before. He was in the bedroom, sprawled in an armchair, gently swigging from a bottle of wine. There was a strange look on his face as he considered what this day meant to him. To his life, his career, his ambitions, his art.

"You can't go like that," Fiona screeched.

Hugh looked down at himself. "It's all I've got."

Fiona walked over to a wardrobe and threw it open to show a rack of Italian suits. "I've bought you hundreds of clothes."

Hugh made a face and turned away. "Let's not start that again. When I buy you hundreds of clothes, then I'll wear the hundreds of clothes you've bought me."

"Well, you've got plenty of money now, go and get yourself some decent gear."

Hugh considered this, then shook his head sadly. "Thing is, it's been so long, I don't know what 'decent' means any more."

2. THE UNVEILING

At the tenement wall dignitaries were gathering. On the stage was Councillor Murphy, wearing his civic chains of office. A short and broad man, he bubbled with bonhomie. Crawford was also there, in uniform. He was a tall man, in his early thirties, with sandy brown hair and the fleshy look of someone who's body just didn't want to be fit. Not fat, but loose, and in every loose fold, nothing. To compensate, he was intelligent, or so he claimed. But that was unfair, he had university degrees, and used long words, and sometimes he even knew what they meant.

The media, in the shape of a TV camera crew, were setting up their cameras, while other less exalted reporters from the newspapers made do with checking the battery levels of their tape recorders by interviewing each other. Murphy looked anxiously at his watch and Crawford said to him , "Can we get this circus on the road ?   I have other 'important' duties, you know."

Murphy looked about, flustered. "He should be here."

Crawford had imagined he was the dignitary for the day. "Who?"

"Hugh Cooper."

"The artist chappie ?" Crawford asked. " Hardly a big deal, he'll have seen the painting."

Murphy put on a pair of thickly lensed glasses and peered down the street. After an agonising wait he croaked, "There he is !"

The old Volvo had seen better days. Fiona, driving, was in a very smartly cut suit, but with a remarkably abbreviated skirt. Hugh, in the passenger seat, was dressed as usual, but had added a bow tie to his ensemble in honour of the occasion.

Fiona reached over and patted Hugh's thigh. "Important day, Hugh. I'm very proud of you.   How do you feel ?"

In reality Hugh felt numb, but knew that some response was expected of him. "See the first time I made love to a girl," he said, "I was still at school.   But I couldn't tell the guys, do the big boasting bit, because I'd been telling them I'd been getting laid for months."

Fiona looked at him quizzically.

"It feels nothing like that," Hugh concluded.

Fiona thought she knew her man. They were getting close to the tenement and there were still words she wanted to hear. "Is there anything you want to say?" she asked,   "About you ... and me?"

The Volvo's exhaust let out a loud bang and the car rolled to a stop. Hugh accepted it with his usual equanimity. "You steer," he answered, "me'll shove."

One hundred yards from the tenement wall which held his destiny Hugh got out of the car and moved behind it to shove it forward. With fifty yards to go the engine spluttered into life. Hugh ran round and climbed into the passenger seat. Fiona drove the last few yards and parked. Hugh got out, very dignified, breathing heavily but trying not to show it.

A civil flunky, in uniform, ran up to try and hustle him onto the stage, but Hugh was having none of it. He escorted Fiona to her seat in the audience before going up on the stage.

He was grabbed almost immediately by Councillor Murphy who raced him round the dignitaries quickly, shaking hands. There were nothing but smiles till he came to Crawford.

"Here's our man of the moment, Superintendent," Murphy said "Hugh Cooper, the artist, please meet Superintendent Crawford Gillespie of Strathclyde Police."

They looked at each other intently.

"Know your face," Crawford said, "Never forget a face."

"Crawford Gillespie?" Hugh mused. "Football? Played against you at school. I was on the right wing, you were the opposing full-back. I ran rings round you."

Crawford's memory was jolted, it all came rushing back to him. "I was played out of position," he complained, "I'm a natural central defender."

Hugh mimed a yawn, but in his head he was there.

"You'll never make a footballer, Hughie, you're too wee. Your legs are too scrawny and your upper body strength wouldn't fill a crisp poke."

"Wee's got nothing to do wi' it. There's skill. What happened to skill? Have I got skill, tell me that?"

"Don't get cheeky, son."

Hugh was playing on the wing, his favourite position, but opposite him was Crawford Gillespie. And Davina was watching, or pretending not to, with a bright ice lolly in her hand.

"There isn't a one-legged full back in the world that would let you by him, Hughie. You'd maybe get a game for Lilliput Rangers."

"Mr Black, you're my coach. You're supposed to gee me up, no' tell me I'm crap."

"Two hundred lines. I shall not say *crap* to a teacher. I'm only trying to save you, wee man. That's the fifteenth time that Crawford Gillespie's kicked you into orbit. It's no' even half time yet, and this is only a friendly, mind."

"I can beat him, sir. I know I can."

The referee was approaching, urging Mr Black to finish his

repairs to Hugh's swollen knee.

"You've beat him every time, son. But he's got longer legs than you. He catches you, and he kicks you. And that's why you're lying here. Why don't you beat him and cross the ball, then he wouldn't have any reason to kick you."

"I'm no' feart o' him."

Mr Black followed Hugh's gaze to the ice lolly, and he grinned sympathetically. He dabbed solidly at Hugh's face with the magic sponge. "You'll never make a footballer, Hughie."

The knee was throbbing, sore to put weight on, but the battle drums were howling their terrible beat, and smoke filled the sky.

Blood was on the ground and pacts had been broken. Swords, unsheathed in anger, demanded their due.

The sky was grey, and a steady, cold, drizzle was half blinding him, but his heart was firm and his hand was steady. The pipes would play no laments for him this night.

"Ho, Captain! Let me ride at the enemy this day, for the runes have been true to me, and the gods shall not let me fail. It is my destiny."

"Don't pass the ball to wee Cooper. He's gone mental!"

But the grail was drawn to him, even as the magic coursed through him. He tapped it lightly, strolling casually over the half-way line, searching the horizon for friend and foe. The shadow of the dreaded Crawford Gillespie fell over him, and he felt his heart tremble, but he laughed at his fear. The shimmy, the jink, the nutmeg, were but minor weapons in his armoury as he danced past.

What? The fiend persisted?

Damn and blast you, man, once more I pass, and again, and again, and again, does shame not pain thee?

And Crawford Gillespie's long leg snaked out, caught Hugh behind the knee and sent him howling into the sky.

Murphy saw the immediate animosity between them and a desire to continue arguing, but managed to drag Hugh away towards the microphone.

"Ladies and gentlemen," Murphy began, "thank you for your patience and welcome to this, the unveiling of the latest of the gable-end murals, commissioned by our city council to brighten up our fair city. We're running a little behind schedule, so I'll go directly to the artist and ask him for a few words. Ladies and gentlemen, one of the city's native treasures, Mr Hugh Cooper."

There was polite applause from all but Fiona who whooped loudly and gave not a fig for the stares this drew.

Davina was in the living room doing her daily stretching routine dressed in a green leotard. She was no fitness freak, but recognised exercise's worth and had made it a habit. She bent to touch her toes, bouncing her repetitions, her behind pointed at the large French windows. A young male window cleaner was polishing the glass with slow circular movements and his total attention on Davina.

Davina noticed him and knew him, the regular guy who'd won the sweep at the window cleaning company to do her windows. She gave him a casual wave before strolling over to draw the curtains, but there was an amused little smile on her face.

Hugh approached the microphone nervously. He pulled a tattered piece of paper from the pocket of his coat, glanced at it and made a face before shoving it away again. He cleared his throat several times.

Finally he said, "Like most artists, I'm not a great one for speaking in public. 'Fact my last appearance was a one-word part. The word was 'guilty' and I must have said it real well, 'cause I got a two month gig out of it."

The audience give a polite little chuckle but Crawford didn't crack a smile.

Hugh, glad that he'd got his joke in, now proceeded at full speed.

"Anyway, I'd like to thank the Council for putting up the money to do the mural. It's important, because the art, if it's any good, has a right to its life; and for the artists concerned, the cash is a desperately needed lifeline. So, thanks for that.

I'm not going to say much about the painting, it should speak for itself, it's about, well .. the mystery that is woman."

Hugh turned to take his seat and there was warmer applause especially from Fiona.

Murphy went up to the microphone. "Thank you for those kind words, Hugh. It's good to know that the Council's commitment to the arts is appreciated. I only wish central government would allow us to release more funds to allow us to do more for our struggling artists. And I don't think it's money that the voters would grudge us spending.

Our arts and our culture are the lifeblood of what we are. They are the statements we leave to posterity .. so don't tell me we should be spending money on slums instead of paintings, this Council is doing both. And doing them both very well, may I add."

Now there was enthusiastic applause from an obviously partisan crowd.

Murphy continued, "So, without further ado, ladies and gentlemen, I am proud to have the honour of unveiling this painting by Hugh Cooper, a work he has entitled, 'The Stormer'."

He turned and pulled a cord. The canvas billowed downward revealing the mural. It was of a voluptuous, attractive, red-haired nude.

There was huge applause and cheering from everybody. People on stage slapped Hugh's back. The camera crew and photographers hurried forward.

Fiona was not applauding or cheering. She stared at the painting, a mean and bitter look on her face. Suddenly she jumped up, grabbed her handbag and headed off towards her car.

Crawford was also not applauding. He looked at the mural, intently and slowly, and realisation dawned. Beneath his breath he whispered, "That's my wife."

Davina, at her house with her friend, Audrey, was putting on her coat, getting ready to go out shopping. Audrey was stylish and highly made-up, whereas Davina was not wearing any make-up. Davina was still, obviously, the better looking of the two.

"Whose car?" Audrey asked.

Davina made a face, "We'll never get parked, the town centre's so busy."

"So we'll get a ticket. What's the point in being married to a cop?"

At the tenement wall the TV crew were filming Hugh standing in front of the mural. Now they closed in so he could be interviewed by the pretty female reporter.

"Well, Hugh," she asked "you know I've got to ask you this, who is it or who's it based on?"

Hugh couldn't help but flirt. "You, sweet thing."

"No, seriously."

It was as if Hugh had never even considered that he'd be asked this question.

"It's not based on anybody," he waffled, "Or it's based on everybody. It's a fantasy, a myth, a creature of the imagination."

But the reporter couldn't leave it alone. "Is she your ideal woman ?"

Hugh gave a little laugh. "The ideal woman doesn't exist any more than the ideal man does."

An older woman, short and dumpy, with her grey hair pulled tightly back, pushed her way forward. "Mr Cooper! Mr Cooper!"

Hugh had an instinctive respect for his elders and gave her his attention. "What can I do for you, Mrs?"

"Rita Reynolds from *The Herald*. Is this the first time you've painted anything on this scale?"

"Naah, this is a miniature compared to what I normally do."

"Humour, Mr Cooper, I like that, I try to do it myself occasionally."

"I've read your column, Rita. You're not bad."

"You're very kind. But is this the biggest piece you've attempted?"

"Just beats the giant papier-mache vibrator I did for the gay pride march by a couple of feet."

"I remember that. Would you let me do a profile of you?"

"If I can do one of you."

Despite her age she was flattered. "Why on Earth would you want to do that?"

"Oh, nothing really, but you've got a face."

Through in the marquee everyone was gathered round the buffet tables, feasting on the food and wine. Crawford searched for Murphy and finally discovered him loading his plate with smoked salmon and cream cheese. He pulled him away from the table roughly. "A quick word, Councillor. Got a bit of a problem."

Murphy had always fancied himself as a bit of a wit. "I'm here to help. I'd be helping the police with their enquiries, I suppose."

He choked on his vol au vent at his own small jest, but Crawford didn't get it.

"A bit awkward really," he coughed. "Thing is, that's my .. eh .. wife .. up there."

Murphy looked at Crawford strangely before walking over to the marquee entrance and staring up at The Stormer. "Good God!" he said finally, "She's certainly a fine looking woman. Bet you didn't have to pay Hugh much to get him to use her as a model, heh heh."

Crawford shook with indignation. "Councillor, I'm not happy about having my wife up there .. in a state of undress .. for all to see."

Realisation dawned slowly on Murphy. "Oh. Of course. Of course not ...... yes, I see ..... of course ..."

Look out there in the glorious City of Glasgow, there's the long, lithe figure of Davina Gillespie playing the plastic.

Spending her man's money.

Buying rubbish.

It's therapy.

And needs investigated.

She's a huntress, stalking a satin blouse down Argyle St; the great white knee-length skirt in Buchanan Galleries; the last known species of cotton jacket in Queen St.

And she's paying next to nothing, the mega-bit bombshell. She's been evaluating stock and prices on a rolling basis for years, can see a SALE coming before the shop assistants.

And it isn't even as if she needs to pay next to nothing. Crawford's earning a healthy salary. They don't smoke, and drink very little. And they don't have any children.

Would that have made a difference?

Davina doesn't care. Playing the plastic is good fun, entertaining, and good exercise too. Time to be yourself.

But there was something funny about today. Something odd.

She noticed people staring at her when she and Audrey stopped for lunch in an Italian restaurant.

Davina was part-used to being stared at, but it was usually lustfully by ambitious young men. This time it was everybody, regardless of age, sex, race, or religion. She checked herself. Her green cord jacket hung over the next chair, nothing wrong with that. The fawn sweater looked okay, no rips or stains, and she was even wearing a bra. The skirt was short for her, but decent in a lighter shade of green than the jacket. It too was unstareable-at. Her legs were bare, but it was a warm day after all.

And her sandals were Italian and expensive, nothing wrong there. What the hell were they staring at?

Was she dressed too young? Or too old?

Yeah, well, too old, but nothing ridiculous. A senior policeman's wife had to maintain certain standards.

Don't come it, Davina. It's your armour.

It had to be her face. What unmentionable was there marring her perfection? She was too angry to be furtive. Grabbed her handbag, took out her small mirror, and looked at herself.

Nothing.

She was as brightly beautiful as she'd ever been.

She put the mirror back in her bag, sipped at her mineral water, and nibbled at her pasta. If it wasn't logical, it wasn't happening.

"Everybody's staring at you," Audrey commented. Audrey was shorter and blonde in a pixieish kind of way, in later life she would be pear-shaped, but now she was just a peach. For her sins she was also opinionated enough to sway dynasties.

"It could be you," Davina replied.

"Nope. Definitely you. You must be firing off pheromones at

a prodigious rate. Bottle some for me."

Davina looked around and thirty people averted their gaze. "God, so they are."

Audrey had finished her lunch and now plunged her fork into Davina's pasta. "Is there anything you should be telling me, Davina?"

"Like what?"

"Well, have you murdered anybody? Slept with your Member of Parliament? Been caught shop-lifting in Paddy's Market?"

Davina lifted Audrey's wine and took a very unladylike slug. "All three, but that's hardly any reason to stare."

"You haven't got your skirt caught in your knickers or anything then?"

"I've checked all that," Davina snapped back. They shrugged it off, finished their lunch and headed back to the hunting.

Audrey was standing by with a saleswoman as Davina tried on a little black party frock. It was short and had a little frill around the hem which danced tantalisingly a she moved. Davina looked at herself in the mirror, watching Audrey's reaction. There was a strange look on Davina's face, pleased but anguished.

"It cannot possibly be wicked," Audrey said, "It is a piece of cloth."

But Davina didn't buy it, it smelt dangerous. She changed back into her own clothes and pulled Audrey out into Buchanan Street. Audrey was loaded down with designer-label bags but noticed that though the precinct was quite busy, people were still turning to stare at them. "I have a feeling your reputation's caught up with you," she commented.

But this time Davina couldn't see it. "I beg your pardon ?"

"Everyone's definitely staring at you, Davina."

Davina looked round but didn't notice anything amiss. "You're being silly."

An old woman, in a faded coat, had been watching their progress. She came over and blocked their path, sticking a grubby piece of paper into Davina's hand.

"Give us your autograph," the old woman demanded, "there's a darling."

Davina shared a horrified look with Audrey, and shoved the bit of paper back in the woman's hand.

But old Glaswegian woman do not take such treatment lying down. "Stuck up bitch !" she screamed after the redhead.

There were wolf-whistles from a bunch of road-diggers gathered round a lorry which forced Davina to ask, "What on Earth is going on ?"

Not far from them a newspaper seller was doing a brisk trade but during a lull he glanced along the length of the precinct and saw the two women walking in his direction. They didn't mean anything to him, but then he did a double-take.. As they reached him he shoved a newspaper into Audrey's hand. She turned to hand it back to him.

"I don't want a newspaper, thank you very much," she intoned icily.

The newspaper guy caught it immediately, their lack of knowledge. "Maybe you don't, but she does."

Audrey looked at the front page of the paper and her eyes went wide. The newspaper seller nodded triumphantly. Audrey pulled the paper away as Davina tried to look.

"Remember how bored you said you were with life?" she said to her friend, "Well, I think that's over. Let's get to the car."

Hugh needed a moment. He managed to sneak away from the crowd and, behind the marquee, lit a cigarette and took long, slow draws, trying to regulate his breathing. Was this it, he wondered? Was this achievement? Was this what he'd strived for? This melee was poor reward. If this was climax it didn't make sense. He shivered at the thought that this was merely foreplay. But Murphy managed to find Hugh and, draping an arm round his shoulder, marched him to Crawford's Audi where he bundled him into the passenger seat.

Ever the politician, he explained his actions smoothly. "Just a quick word with the Superintendent, Hugh. Won't take long."

Hugh looked over at the gaunt man and with an instinctive distrust of authority said warily, "You're right. You were played out of position."

Crawford was not amused but very businesslike. It was his way.

"That's my wife up there," he said.

This threw Hugh to the ground and assaulted him with confusion. Slowly, but slowly, the truth dawned on him. "God, so it was you she married," he finally blurted out.

Crawford leapt on this admission. "So you do know her?"

Hugh took a deep breath and tried to explain. "We went to the same school. Fancied her like mad, but she had no time for me. Had the hots for some police cadet. You."

Crawford was not appeased by this admission that he'd won the maiden. "It won't do. You'll have to paint it over or change it or something."

Hugh realised now that this was more serious than he'd imagined. The anger rose in him.

"No way. That's The Stormer. The way she has to be. You might have married her, but that doesn't change anything."

Crawford was used to uncooperative people. He prodded at Hugh with his car keys.

"I'm a fairly important person in this town, Mr Cooper," he threatened, "and I have many influential friends. I can make life very awkward for you. And I can go right over your head to the Council to have this abomination removed."

Crawford had just pushed the wrong button.

"Abomination ? Kiss my artistic arse," Hugh spat. He turned to Murphy. "You tell him."

Hugh got out of the car and slammed the door behind him.

Crawford looked at the tubby Councillor with a suspicious eye. "Tell me what, Councillor?"

Murphy had brought his food and drink with him and had been happily munching away while Hugh and Crawford spoke to each other. Now he had to swallow quickly.

"There's not a great deal we can do about it. We don't .. eh.. actually own it."

"You paid for it. You made a very boring speech about paying for it."

Murphy smiled stupidly. "It's a great scheme, recommended by the accountants. We haven't bought it, we've leased it. For 25 years. Spreads the cost, you see. After that we can buy it. For a penny."

"So there's nothing you can do?"

Murphy nodded. "It's a very good picture. It was approved by the arts sub-committee."

"I'm sure it was," Crawford said, "I'll have to sort out this degenerate painter some other way then." He started the engine, then gruffly turning round. "Get out of my car, Murphy."

Hugh strode down the pedestrian precinct of Sausage Roll Street avoiding the cars. He often wondered about Sausage Roll Street because it was undoubtedly the most famous thoroughfare in Glasgow. It was mentioned in every book he'd ever read about Glasgow, even ones that only gave the city a passing nod.

Why?

There was nothing to it. It was just another point A to point B space between buildings. Nothing special.

And this made him wonder about other famous thoroughfares. Were they just as boring? Hugh had never stepped out of his golden city, he didn't know. He had a suspicion they were all just as dull, another con. Champs Elysee, Broadway, a swizz.

Such is life.

He'd just come away from the unveiling ceremony and was heading for the Dog's Breath.

"Do you know you're on the world-famous Sausage Roll Street, missus?"

"Help, don't look at me like that, that's terminal."

"Do ye even know you're alive?"

The worst thing about cheap wine is it slips down like cola and gives ye a raging thirst before you've even had the chance to have a decent hangover. No justice.

Thank God none of the boys had turned up at the unveiling. A surprise considering the free drink. It was a strange world where grown men turned up the chance of free drink.

An abomination, and a plague on their houses, bless them.

Where had all this sunshine come from, the winter would be here soon enough and this was Glasgow for crying out loud. People just didn't have the wardrobe to cope with these unnatural conditions. Look at that fella, just the bottom button of his overcoat done up, an' his chest hairs wafting in the breeze.

"Hey Jimmy, how come ye don't just take the coat off as well?"

"Sorry, didn't realise you weren't wearing trousers either."

And they reckoned this place could be the fashion capital o' Europe. That'll be right.

Hugh hopped for ten yards.

That always gets people looking at you. Funny, you'd think they'd never seen anybody hopping before. Christ, it's in the Olympics, hen. That and synchronised wife swapping. And the Mormons would have a head start on that one.

When he got there the Dog's Breath was busy, though not as busy as the previous night. Fiona was sitting at a table with Midden, nursing an elaborate cocktail. Hugh came in and there was a noticeable drop in the level of the ambient conversation. Hugh went to the bar, got himself a drink and brought it over to the table. Midden nodded wisely and wandered off to join some other bikers at the bar while Hugh sat down.

"You disappeared," Hugh said.

"Yeah, right off the wall," and her voice sliced like a blade.

Hugh had been smiling, now he looked puzzled. "What?"

"Who is the cow?"

"Who?"

"That bitch in the painting."

"Oh hell, is that what's bothering you ? She's a nobody, a fantasy."

Fiona raised her voice. "It was meant to be me, you shit. It was about the mystery of woman, you said it, and now you've made me look like an utter clown."

The enormity of his naivety hit Hugh. He looked skyward, closed his eyes, praying.

"Oh, dear God, why can't I do anything right ? I honestly thought that my girlfriend, Fiona, wouldn't want to be painted, naked, 20 feet high, on a gable-end wall. I was trying to relate to her feelings, especially as she's sensitive about her job."

"I am not a tart!" Fiona screamed.

"See what I mean," Hugh offered the deity.

Over with the bikers, Midden was winding them up. "That little bastard has done you out of seeing my sister in the buff, what do you make of that?"

The bikers looked towards Hugh and growled.

"You told me we'd get married the minute you had money," Fiona attacked.

"I've had the cheque just over twenty four hours." Hugh explained,   "and I've been busy.

"With that big, tarty, red-head, I suppose."

"This is supposed to be a happy day for me, Fifi, and you're ruining it."

Fiona swallowed her drink and picked up her bag. "You aint seen nothing yet, pal."

And with that she blazed out and Hugh feared for his very soul.

Rita Writes:

Commuters heading into Glasgow city centre from the west, along Dumbarton Road or the Clydeside Expressway are in for a treat. From yesterday they will have a wonderful piece of art to enjoy on a gable end wall at the Thornwood roundabout.

To say it is stunning would be an understatement; it is quite simply the finest painting these old eyes have seen for many a year.

This masterpiece is titled The Stormer and is the work of Glasgow born Hugh Cooper, who has been on the fringes of Glasgow's arts scene for a good many years.

The Stormer is the latest in the City Council's attempts to smarten up the city, but in sheer quality it far outshines what has gone before.   The Stormer, and it is a she, is a stunningly beautiful redheaded nude, reclining on a bed, confident and revelling in her beauty. It is sensual, erotic, inspiring, and a credit to its artist.

At the unveiling yesterday Hugh denied that the painting was based on any one person, but was in fact 'a fantasy, a myth, or a creature of the imagination'. If that is the case, Hugh Cooper has an incredible imagination, and why he hasn't found recognition before now is a mystery. Take it from me, Hugh Cooper is an artist we will be seeing a lot more of.

Cllr Peter Murphy, chair of the Council committee responsible for selecting the works which have appeared on the city's walls, had this to say, "Glasgow is a large city with s diverse community and it is our job to reflect that. Hugh's work tells us what he believes in, but may not necessarily reflect the views of all Glaswegians. But, living in a democracy, we must defend his right to hold his views."

Cllr Murphy denied that he was making this statement in an attempt to avoid any kind of moral backlash. He said, "The nudity is not an issue, and there is nothing offensive in this painting. We are living in the 21st Century."

And Hugh, when asked if he'd deliberately set out to be controversial had this to say, "I don't do controversial, I do art. It's for the viewer to find it offensive or otherwise. But in my eyes The Stormer is a beautiful woman and anyone who finds that offensive is off his head."

The Stormer joins Kids Playing, Glencoe Snowstorm, The Dancers and Fireworks Night as one of the murals now adorning Glasgow.

The anger of a woman scorned has been commented on in many places, yet for all its terrors it is rarely an uncalculated fury. Fiona's was.

She went directly home and straight to the kitchen where she found a large pair of scissors. Entering the bedroom she threw open the wardrobe and attacked Hugh's suits. Legs and sleeves went flying and single breasted became double breasted with one flash of steel before she stopped, sobbing, slumped to her knees and remembered that she had paid for the suits.

There was a very limited number of items in the flat that were irrevocably Hugh's and for a moment Fiona was stumped. But then she remembered and knew how best to hurt him. There was a little cupboard off the hallway, where Hugh stored his paintings. Fiona pulled them out, one by one, and stabbed at them with her scissors, in a frenzy.

Davina was sitting on the sofa sipping coffee. The newspaper was lying on the coffee table. The headline read 'NEW MURAL IN LINE FOR EURO AWARD'.

Davina lifted the paper, took it to a mirror and held it up to see both her reflection and the photograph. There could be no doubts about the inspiration behind the painting.

She heard the front door opening and eventually Crawford came in. He was all smiles, but they disappeared when he saw that she had a newspaper.

"Ahh. You know," was his only comment.

Davina smiled wanly. "I would imagine the whole world does."

She threw the paper aside and asked, "But why aren't the hacks at my door?   The only phone call I've had was from my mum. She thought I looked well in the paper, but was worried in case I'd caught a cold."

"We won't have any trouble from the press chappies. They were duty bound to cover the unveiling of this thing, but there's no connection with us. I've had a word." Crawford reassured.

"What the hell is going on, Crawford?" Davina asked.

"I assume from your tone that you never posed for this thing?"

"Do me a favour," she said sardonically, "I've never even heard of this ..." She picked up the paper and scanned it again ".... Hugh Cooper?"

But her face betrayed the fact that, as she said the name aloud, memories were being stirred.

"He claims to have known you at school," Crawford said.

She shook her head, then suddenly smiled. "Hugh Cooper? The Coop! The wee bugger made it.   And I thought he'd end up a sign-writer."

"So you do know him.   That's unfortunate, it'll do my career prospects no great good to have my wife the acquaintance of a known pervert."

Davina rebuked him mildly. "He's hardly a pervert."

Crawford came over and kissed her chastely on the forehead. "You're awfully naive, Davina dear, though personally I find it rather endearing.   What's for dinner?"

3. IT BEGINS

After a night in the bar it is the wont of Glaswegian gentlemen to partake of a little sustenance before retiring, so Hugh went to a chip shop when he left the Dog's Breath.

Standing in the queue he noticed that he had attained an aura of invisibility as others, on both sides of him in the queue, were being served briskly by two plump girls.

"Pies?" Hugh asked.

He was ignored by the girls and beckoned over the owner.

Mario folded his arms and looked at him defiantly. "Sorry, no pies. Late delivery."

"Fish?"

"They're on strike."

"Pizza?"

"Pizza off."

Hugh pointed to the guy preceding him. "He got a pizza."

"It was the last one."

"Am I barred or something?" Hugh asked.

Mario gave him a warm smile. "Barred? You? Hugh, you are my old friend!" He gestured Hugh over with a jerk of his head. "Tonight," he whispered, "Once we are closed. Come to the back door. I might manage something."

"What? Am I contagious or something? Be a man and serve me where everybody can see me."

"That I cannot do, but I would not let you starve." He said it with a wink.

Hugh appreciated the gesture but could not resist the legendary retort of the unwanted. "Stick your chips up your arse!"

Crawford pulled on his old, striped pyjamas and before getting into his bed, which was separate from his wife's, he felt the need to make a little speech.

"I have been stimulated by it," he said, "I admit to that, I am human. But because I am human, and not one of the lesser animals, I do not succumb to temptation. We do not behave like beasts in the field, that is what makes us superior."

Having got that off his chest he climbed into the single bed. Davina sat on hers, above the covers, propped up by pillows, reading a book. She was wearing a shortish, satin, nightie and looked very attractive. She ignored his little rant.

Crawford lay rigid for a moment, looking over at her, then suddenly whipped his hands out from under the duvet and placed them chastely on top.

Within minutes he was snoring with the erratic frequency of a foghorn and it annoyed Davina to the extent that she gave up reading. She switched off the bedside lamp and swung herself under her own covers. Somehow she knew she wouldn't find sleep easy and so it proved.

Hugh Cooper?

The Stormer?

What did it all mean?

She was a married woman, the wife of a policeman, living a humdrum life in suburbia, these things shouldn't be happening to her. The whole thing had obviously upset Crawford, but she wasn't to blame. Hugh Cooper had just been a non-entity in her childhood and yes he'd had a crush on her, but so what? She turned to lie on her right side and pulled her knees up. She'd have to go and look at this painting, see what all the fuss was about. If it really annoyed Crawford she'd complain to the Council, she must have some rights. But it was just so typical of the boy-idiot Hugh she remembered, to pull a stunt like this, to paint her nude. She grinned to herself and turned onto her left side. She must have made a more powerful impression on him than she'd thought. He was the same age as her and should be married and settled down by now, not painting pictures of girls he'd known at school. He must be mad. That would fit the profile of the boy she remembered. A wee nutcase. She drifted off and found herself elsewhere.

She was winning Miss World.

She was winning an Olympic Gold for swimming.

She was a princess.

She was a supermodel.

She was washing dishes while her mother made dinner. It was mince and tatties and her mother was slicing carrots into the mince.

"Aye, your Dad loves his mince," her mother said, "and if he doesn't get it on a Tuesday there'll be hell to pay."

Davina knew her mother was exaggerating, her father was a sweet man who never raised his voice. He was a good and decent man and she loved him. He was a working class Glaswegian and worked in a shipyard, but even coming home drunk on a Friday night he would be soft-spoken and gentle.

Davina knew that all men, all fathers, weren't like that, she had friends who suffered from loud and violent abuse when the men came home with a wasted pay packet, but for all his proletarian credentials her father was a gentleman. And he wouldn't go wild if he didn't get mince on a Tuesday. It was her mother's sense of humour.

"Maybe we should give him stew," Davina said, "just to wind him up."

"Have you got a death wish, pet?"

"We're awful stuck in our ways, mum, with mince and tatties every Tuesday and sausage casserole on Wednesday and …."

"You wait till you're cooking your man's dinner every night, you'll fall into a routine too. It just makes life easier, that's all. When your Dad and I first got married I'd ask him every morning what he wanted for his tea that night and it used to drive him demented. 'Just make whatever you want,' he'd say and so that's what I did. Saved him from having to think and eventually, once Id set up the routine, it saved me from having to think too."

"But don't you fancy something different now and again."

"We've all got mouths to speak with. If your Dad wants something fancy, he can ask. Or is it you that's getting bored?"

"No, mum, I love your mince. I love all your cooking."

"You're biddable, Davina, I'll give you that. Just don't make yourself so soft that people shove you around."

"Nobody shoves me around. They know my Dad would set about them."

"Aye, he would that. You're his wee treasure."

Davina came and stood against her mother. "Not so wee, I'm taller than you and nearly as big as him."

Her mother pushed her away. "God knows where you get that from."

"Aliens," Davina said. "I think you and dad adopted me, same as Clark Kent."

"Is he in your class?"

"Superman, Mum. He was born on Krypton and was sent to Earth when it was going to blow up, and the Kents adopted him."

28

"Oh, so now you're Superman?"

"Well, Supergirl, maybe."

"You're a blether."

Damn, her mother had discovered her true identity, Blethergirl, who captured villains by talking them into submission.

She remembered when she'd faced the deadly Shevil, Mistress of Doom, and had to talk non-stop for three and a half hours before her foe submitted. She'd saved the city but the Mayor wouldn't give her any more awards because her thank you speeches tended to go on a bit. That was gratitude for you.

There had never been a woman on the moon, she wouldn't mind doing that. Or was she too tall for a space suit? She wasn't sure if she liked being taller than all her friends. It made her stand out and essentially she was shy. Too shy to be up on a gable end wall. With no clothes on too. That was rude. She'd have to get her Dad to go and see that little shit, Hugh Cooper. Her Dad would sort him out. And then they would have tatties and mince. It was Tuesday after all.

Rita Writes:

Last week I told you of The Stormer, a painting by Glasgow's own Hugh Cooper. Having met him at the unveiling of his piece I found him to be an interesting character and worthy of further investigation. So, this old lady hitched up her girdle and made her way to the Dog's Breath Bar which is seemingly Hugh's General Headquarters. I found him there, not in an alcoholic stupor as I'd expected, for he is after all an artist, but painting the pub's ceiling. He was doing this to pay off an outstanding bar bill, though he had now received payment for The Stormer, and could well cancel his debt with cash. As he said, "I've got nothing else to do," and note that I've removed an expletive.

The question is, why? Why does this thirty four year old native son, trained at the Glasgow School of Art, who has undoubtedly been touched by genius, have to paint pubs to pass his time? Where are the commissions for further work which should be his due?

"It's because The Stormer is popular," according to Hugh, and he may well have hit on a damning truth there. The Stormer's very popularity and the public accolades it has received have marked it down, in the eyes of the artistic cognoscenti at least, as the work of a lesser talent.

"It's part of the game and I accept it," Hugh added, "I have a skill and I hope to use that skill to earn a living. Nothing else matters. Fame, acclaim, they're all tosh. Give me the money."

This attitude horrified me, for it seemed to imply that Hugh had given up hoping for the fame he should rightfully have, and was willing to settle for a workman's wage when he should have that of a master craftsman. But Hugh would have none of that.

"I could take the shilling," he said, "go and work for some advertising agency as a graphic designer or whatever, but I don't work on a screen, I work on a canvas. And occasionally a wall. Sure, I'm hungry for money, but I'm my own master and only paint what I want to, not what somebody else tells me to."

I countered that this was a fanciful notion, that in the end run we all had to bow to some kind of market forces. Even I, with my years of writing this column, have to bow to the will of an editor, though I admit I'm allowed certain liberties.

"You got lucky," Hugh said, "I bet there are better writers, better newshounds, better columnists, than you out there who aren't making a fraction of what you're earning. It happens everywhere, writers, artists, actors, all the skill in the world and damned for the lack of a stroke of luck. Shakespeare got it right with his 'tide in the affairs of men'."

I couldn't dispute this but sought to regain some measure of pride by insisting that I must have some qualities which my employers found to be worthy of my remuneration, but the artist would have none of it. "Luck," he insisted, "Nothing but bloody luck. Am I a better painter now than I was five years ago? No, but nobody would spit on me then and now they're drawing round like flies. Don't get me wrong, I may be painting a pub ceiling, but I've had plenty of offers now my name's in the paper, but it's hack work and not what I fancy doing."

I left him feeling that this man was dangerous for he was armed with the truth and unafraid to speak it, or to paint it. I shall be keeping an eye on him.

Hugh bore the hunger of the drunk like a man. He climbed up the stairs and reached the landing of the place he'd recently called home. Two suitcases, carelessly crammed with Hugh's clothes and effects were lying outside Fiona's door. An easel lay atop them. Scattered around were his destroyed paintings.
Hugh shook his head sadly, lifted a painting, an obvious favourite, and groaned.
He'd always fancied himself for eloquence, but all he could manage now was a despairing, "No, no, no, no."

The next morning dawned grey and chilly and various people stopped to look at The Stormer. There were businessmen, school kids, shoppers. There was no response of disgust or shock from anyone. They looked, smiled faintly, and nodded in approval. They appreciated the art.
As the grey of the morning retreated and the sun burst through the clouds like a bombshell, a small blue Toyota drew up at the kerb. For half an hour a woman, with headscarf, dark glasses and upturned coat collar, sat in the driver's seat, watching The Stormer's passing audience.
Eventually she and her friend got out of the car.
Davina and Audrey, along with a hundred others, stood and stared up at The Stormer. The disguise was no Hollywood affectation, Davina Gillespie was indeed shy.
"Whoa, someone does have an admirer," Audrey said.
"It's beautiful," Davina breathed.
"You're beautiful." Audrey, confident in her own qualities, could say that to another woman without pause.
"That's not me. That's something .. something .. strange .. unworldly .."
Audrey read from a newspaper she'd brought. "Artist says it's the way he sees you ... a tribute to first love ...but then he denies it's based on anybody in particular."
Davina squinted. "Maybe it isn't me."
Audrey shaded her eyes with the paper. "Are you fucking

blind? Of course it's you. Look, the left tit's slightly bigger than the right, same as yours."

"Bitch!" Davina hissed unvenomously.

"So who have you been showing your tits to, lady?"

"Nobody!" and then sadly, "Except Crawford."

Audrey grinned. "Well, this Cooper guy certainly had the hots for you."

"But that was years ago, we were at school."

"Big torch to carry. Must have been running on Duracell."

Attention was turning to them. It was warm in the sunshine and the headscarf was a bit of a giveaway, she peeled it off. As she felt the approval, she slowly took off her shades and shook out her flaming mane.

Everybody was smiling. A doddery old woman patted Davina on the shoulder, a 'well-done' sign.

Audrey took Davina's arm and led her back to the main road. "Oh my, my," she said happily, "we *are* living in exciting times."

In the way of such things Hugh had been forced into sleeping on a park bench. He woke now, cold and stiff and slapped his arms to try and warm up. He stretched himself and flexed his muscles.

The scruffiest tramp in the world, Shame by name and Shame by nature, wandered up and watched Hugh's contortions. He took a tattered old notebook from his pocket and started writing as he approached the artist. "You got a union card ?" he asked.

"Piss off!" Hugh replied.

Shame staggered back from the power of this verbal rebuff, but rallied himself.

"Abuse will get you nowhere," he insisted, "If we want a civilised society, we must have rules. It's only five pounds to join and you get all the benefits."

Hugh shrugged him away and obeyed the commands of his growling stomach by heading for the nearest café where the full fry up assailed his nostrils deliciously.

Hugh found an empty table at the window, but within seconds a waitress appeared and removed the plastic sauce bottles, the condiment set, the menu and the cutlery. Hugh watched her, bewildered.

When she returned he had hardly opened his mouth to say, "Excuse me…" when she planked a 'RESERVED' sign down on the table. Hugh realised what was going on, once again he was becoming invisible, and shook his head. Once again he repeated his mantra, "No, no, no, no ......"

He accepted the inevitable and left the cafe just as a black hack with its 'Hire' sign lit drove by. Hugh had nowhere particular to go but tried to flag it down and the driver slowed, but at the last moment his eyes locked with Hugh's and he quickly pulled away. Again, "No, no, no, no ...."

The tramp, Shame, had followed Hugh and now came up to him and put an arm around his shoulders.

"I see a kindred spirit in anguish and my heart is moved," he said, "Society has branded you a leper, a situation not unlike my own. Come, fellow, tell me your woes."

Hugh carefully removed Shame's arm and looked him up and down.

"How would you like to earn that fiver?" Hugh asked.

Shame hung his head coyly and fluttered his eyelashes. "I'm not that kind of a chap."

Hugh gestured to Shame to follow him with a flick of his head.

"No, no' that. You look like the kind of fella who's seen a bit of action in his day. The forces maybe?"

"You are a great judge of men," the Shame agreed, "but I never served under the flag of my country. I am, however, a black belt with a sawn off shotgun." The tramp held out a crusty hand and cocked an eyebrow. "They call me The Shame, a Glasgow man, by birth and by nature."

"Good, I need a painting guarded." Hugh saw the way the wind was blowing and knew that if his sudden invisibility was Crawford's work then the lunatic was having a go at him and would attempt war on The Stormer as well.

His orders had an invigorating effect on Shame. He lifted his chin and his shambling gait became a march. They started walking towards the tenement wall.

But Crawford had beaten them to it. He stood and stared up at the mural. How had Cooper captured that essence of her? She gave more to the world in that painting than she'd ever given to Crawford in the flesh. He was alive enough to know that, and it hurt. He felt the urge to get up and touch the painting, knowing that there would only be cold brick there for him, but it would be more than he'd ever had.

But he was too tired, too weary, too drained. Any deviation from the rail tracks of his life cost him dearly.

A police van was parked in the street and two young constables were taking traffic-cones from the back of it and placing them in the street, blocking access to the city park and keeping viewers of The Stormer at a distance. Crawford stood by the van with Sergeant Watt, nodding sagely. "What do you think of my ruse, Watt?"

"As long as there aren't any repercussions."

"Repercussions? I have a duty to maintain public safety."

One of the constables approached him and asked, "Are you sure, sir?"

"'Course I am, man. Possible fractured gas main. Somebody gives it a funny look and ... kaboom!"

The constable returned to his partner, nodded up at the painting and winked.

Hugh saw them from a distance and stopped. He pointed towards the mural. "Do you see that?" he asked Shame.

"Perfectly, it is a woman person, divested of her raiment, and a joy to the beholder, if I may so."

"I painted that."

A strange, glazed look came into Shame's eyes. "You are more than I thought," he said, and he sounded lucid.

"What do you think of her?" Hugh asked the Shame.

"Is she gloss or emulsion? Or should that be oil or watercolour?"

"But there are wankers out there that don't like her and want to destroy her," Hugh continued.

"A curse on the Philistines."

"So I want you to hang about here and keep an eye on my girl. If you see any ladders or scaffolding going up, you phone me right away. Here's the number of the pub I hang out in. If I'm not there, leave a message."

"I don't have to engage them in combat or anything?"

"No, just phone me." He took a ten pound note and stuffed it into Shame's dirt ingrained hand. "Don't let me down."

The Shame saluted, "Never, my Captain."

Hugh clapped him on the back and walked off to discover what other mischief Crawford had sorted out for him.

4. PLANS

They were in his office and Crawford, seated behind his desk, believed he was secure in discussing the pressing issues of the day with Sgt Watt. Watt had once been a mentor to Crawford, but in his role of whiz-kid he'd far surpassed the older man.

"I will not go off half-cocked," he said and there seemed to be some method in his madness.

Watt who had no idea what his boss was talking about said, "Of course not, sir."

"That would be an elementary mistake and I will not make it. Planning, we will have planning. Planning and structured application."

"Masterful, sir. But what precisely are you talking about?"

"The Hugh Cooper situation," Crawford grunted, "He must be stopped in his tracks before he corrupts the whole city."

"Cooper? Haven't heard of him. Drugs, is it?"

"No, no, man, he's the obscene artist chappie who's painted that damn thing along Dumbarton Road, the bit we coned off."

"Oh yes, have there been further complaints?"

"Don't worry about that, I'm a citizen, I can make a complaint."

"Oh, so it's personal, sir?"

"Don't be ridiculous."

Crawford scattered sheets of paper across his desk and with a red felt marker headed them with words such as Aims, Objectives, Applications and Actions.

"Do you want him arrested, Superintendent?"

Crawford considered this. "That is one of the options open to us and I shall bear it in mind, but I'm really more concerned with utterly destroying this man."

"Destroying? Surely that's a bit severe, sir."

"Not at all, he deserves it."

"For painting a wall?"

"It's what the painting is of, Watt."

"Oh, your wife?"

That stopped Crawford in his tracks. "Does it? Does it look like my wife?" he asked, lifting his chin in mock surprise.

Watt picked his teeth. "Common knowledge, sir. Talk of the steamie even. I would estimate that eighty percent of the Glaswegian population know that the Stormer painting is of a policeman's wife and at least half of those know that it is of your wife specifically."

"Really. Well that puts a different perspective on things. Some people might think I was pursuing this man out of a sense of personal vengeance."

"Whereas that couldn't possibly be the case."

"Of course not. But it means I must play a very remote part in proceedings where possible."

"I don't see that we can do much more than arrest him."

"Ahh, Watt, that displays your lack of imagination and shows why you are still a Sergeant while I am a Superintendent."

"Yes, sir."

"No, no, I think we must adopt a multi-pronged attack on this miscreant." He began furiously scribbling on the sheets of papers he'd scattered.

"Desirable outcome one, exile," he muttered to himself. "Achieved by.." He looked up at Watt like an expectant schoolteacher, "By?"

"Sorry?"

"How do we achieve the exile of Mr Hugh Cooper, accepting that we cannot bodily kick him outwith the city limits."

Watt drummed his fingers on Crawford's desk as he pondered this. Eventually he said, "Make life uncomfortable for him, I suppose."

"Excellent. We have started to make life very uncomfortable for Mr Cooper and we shall continue. That will be a task for you, Watt. There are certain areas where we can exercise some of our powers, but in a subtle way, and I need you to go and see certain people and drop large hints. Can you do that?"

"Drop hints. I think I can manage that."

"Good, good. But everything must be hush hush, there must be no paperwork on this entire affair.

Watt's jaw dropped. No paperwork? It went against everything he'd learned in his twenty five years of police service. "But I can't operate without paperwork, sir. I don't know how."

Crawford swung his feet upon his desk. "Very well, you may use paperwork for operational purposes, but it must be destroyed once each phase is complete and while it exists it must never be traceable to this office."

"Each phase," Watt asked weakly.

"The secret of my success, Watt, is anticipation. Say we expend all our energies in dislodging Mr Cooper by making him uncomfortable and he doesn't budge. We look rather foolish then, don't we?"

It was rhetorical but Watt gave it a solemn nod.

"So we anticipate, and have alternative strategies in place, ready to be implemented the minute we face possible failure and thus avoid egg on face."

"Very clever, sir."

"Now, as you know, I have already taken some action against the painting itself as a parallel action to your Operation Uncomfortable. We shall put these into motion and then extend our strategic map to encounter whatever comes our way. Is that clear?"

"I think so, sir."

"Well, get on with it."

"Get on with what, sir?"

"Your part of the plan, which I've already put into motion, bar Hugh Cooper from Glasgow."

The Dog's Breath had just opened and the cleaner was still mopping the floor. There were no customers in yet as Hugh entered and marched up to the bar where Bob was fiddling about in the till.

"And don't you tell me you're not serving me either," Hugh said.

Bob turned and looked about in every direction but Hugh's. "Where did that noise come from?" he asked no-one.

Deprived of food and drink, Hugh played a wild card and headed off to Fiona's place of work.

He entered the massage parlour and the girl at the reception desk frantically moved fashion magazines to get at her panic button and hit it.

Hugh kept striding forward as the establishment's large and bulky minder came out of a side room and tried to block his path. Hugh didn't slow his stride but took a small paintbrush from an inside pocket and poked the steward in the eye with the sharp end as he ducked by him.

In her lair Fiona was perched up on the massage couch, her legs crossed, painting her fingernails, as Hugh entered. She looked down at him and sneered, "You are persona non grata, little artist person, not wanted on voyage. You have got up the nose of some big-shot cop and he has put out the word on you. Consumer & Trading Standards, Environmental Health, Weights & Measures, they're all in it together. They've been round and everybody that needs a license to operate has been told - 'do not do business with Hugh Cooper'."

"Just a cup of coffee," Hugh pleaded, "we need to talk."

Fiona was having none of it. "You're threatening my livelihood just standing there. The question is, what have you done to this cop that's got him so upset?"

Hugh shook his head and turned back to the door. "Well, if there's no coffee going. And thanks for the demolition job on my stuff."

The bottle of nail polish came flying by his head to strike the door, leaving a pleasing streak of pearlescent pink.

"I'm upset already, Hugh. Answer the question, what have you been up to?"

Hugh was caught and didn't know which way to wriggle. Fiona's eyes bored into him and forced him to honesty. "It's this cop's missus," he mumbled, "The Stormer. I didn't know. Honest."

Fiona's smile was deadly. "I was just starting to feel sorry for you," she seethed, "was going to let you back into my life. And now I find you painting other women behind my back."

"It's not like that."

"A senior police officer's wife too? Are you entirely stupid?"

38

And deep in his heart, Hugh knew he was.

Coning off the street wasn't enough, Crawford decided. He couldn't extend his exclusion zone far enough without questions being raised upstairs. People could still see The Stormer, albeit at not more than postage stamp size, but it still irked him. After considerable thought he decided that if he couldn't destroy the damn thing or keep people away from it he would have to mask it. Consequently he visited a shop specialising in equipment for discos and clubs and bought the largest smoke machine that money could buy. To run it he also had to hire a generator, but eventually he managed to get the equipment in place and fired up. A healthy cloud of smoke soon appeared and Crawford was celebrating his genius when the wind picked up and in that battle between machine and nature, nature wins.

But it took more than nature to thwart the plans of a police Superintendent. Crawford called upon the services of one of the criminal classes he so despised. One of the groups of young tearaways who were just on the cusp of graduating to the position of hardened criminals.

"It's a simple job, Slab," he explained.

"Good, boss. I like simple," the giant replied. "Do I get to punch somebody? I like punching people. I like to see them falling down."

"No, Slab. You don't need to punch anybody, all I want you to is get some of your little chums together and paint a gable end wall."

"Paint?" Slab who had notions of being a criminal mastermind was insulted. "We don't do painting, Mr Gillespie. It's not that we're exactly specialists but me and the boys prefer a bit of robbing, grievous bodily harm, that kind of stuff."

"I know, I know, Slab," Crawford consoled, "but this job doesn't require any of your specialities, just the painting of an exterior wall in the dead of night, without being seen. A bit of a guerrilla job."

Slab looked wary. "Is it a favour? Cause you know the rules, if it's a favour and we get caught, we blab. You pay us, it's not a favour, it's a job of work and our honour means our lips are sealed."

Crawford reached for his wallet and said, "That was very eloquently put, Slab, and does great credit to your profession. It is a job and there will be wages."

"How much?"

"One hundred pounds." And he pulled a sheaf of notes from his wallet and flourished them before the bulky man.

"Gable end? That's going to take five guys. Two hundred. Each."

"Good God, man, that's a thousand pounds!"

"Crime has to pay, Mr Gillespie, or nobody would do it."

Crawford made rapid calculations. It would be worth it. "Okay, but I don't have it all on me. Here's three hundred and you get the rest when the job's done."

Slab took the money and counted it methodically. "What about the paint?"

"Oh, you'll have to deal with that, I don't have the time."

Slab cleared his throat. "Bit of a problem there, Mr Gillespie. Me and the boys are barred from every DIY shop in Glasgow. Some problems with accusations of shoplifting. Totally unfounded, of course."

"Oh bugger."

"And we'll need ladders … and brushes … and overalls."

"Listen, man, I'm not setting you up in a new career."

"Can't do the job without the proper tools."

Crawford saw the whole scheme spiralling out of control cost-wise, but it was his dogged determination which had got him so far in his career. "Very well, I'll supply everything."

"What colour?"

"What?"

"The paint, what colour?"

"What on Earth has that got to do with anything? I just want the wall painted over."

Slab nodded slowly, superior in his decorating knowledge. "At night?" he asked.

"Yes, this has to be done in utmost secrecy."

"So what if it's black paint? You can't see black paint in the dark."

"Yes, yes, light pink then."

"Which won't cover and you'll need two coats for a decent finish."

"There won't be time for two coats."

"For one coat we need dark paint. If we use dark paint we need lights. If we use lights, we'll be seen."

Crawford followed the logic precisely but was unimpressed. "My dear Slab, The important thing in this plan is that what is currently on the wall is no longer seen, not that we achieve a perfect finish."

Slab looked disappointed. "Can't fault a man for taking pride in his work, boss."

Crawford scribbled on a sheet from his notepad and passed it to Slab. "Very well, I'll get the stuff and meet you at this address tomorrow at midnight."

Slab took the slip and folded it neatly with the cash before slipping them into his pocket.

Crawford stood up and headed for the door. He turned as he reached it and said, "I don't expect you chaps would accept a cheque?"

"Oh, you are a wag, Mr Gillespie," Slab chuckled.

It was the first time in his life that Crawford had ever been considered witty.

Having failed to win sympathy from his girlfriend, Hugh turned for aid to her brother. Midden ran a small motorcycle garage. Little more than a lock-up, it was dirty and crammed with motorcycles and spares and wasn't much more than a daytime hang-out for Midden's biker pals. This capitalist endeavour allowed Midden to exercise some radical commercial principles. Midden sourced parts for bikes needing repairs by riding around in a van and looking for a suitable donor model parked conveniently and then throwing it in the back of the van. In his eyes he was recycling.

"A cop's woman, jeeze," he replied to Hugh's explanation of events.

"He's put the word out on me," Hugh continued, "I'm barred ... from everywhere. Not a bus, a taxi, an off-license, a pub or a corner shop'll serve me.   I can't even get a shave within the city limits."

"Were you giving her one?" Midden asked, eager for salacious detail.

"You're worse than your sister," Hugh grunted,   "No, I was not giving her one.   She was a girl I knew at school.   A crush.   Dead innocent.   She didn't reckon me, and I haven't seen her in over fifteen years."

This insanity didn't suit Midden's prosaic way of looking at things. "So why the hell did you paint her on that wall and burst Fiona's arse?"

"I don't know anymore. It seemed right at the time.   Shit, I'm an artist, I don't have to justify the work."

Midden gave up working on his bike, threw a spanner to the ground and stood up.

"Me and the boys went to see the painting. She's some looking babe, your Stormer, a special fish supper, no doubt about it."

The compliment passed Hugh by. "Thing is, what do I do about this loony cop?"

Midden considered for a moment, wiping the grease from his hands onto a rag.

"Oh, that's no problem."

Hugh smiled and looked at the hulking bikers larking about in the back.

"Thank Christ, you think the guys'll help me?" he asked, relieved.

Midden shook his head and pushed Hugh gently towards the street. In the end run he was a pragmatist. "Not at all.   Just you trot down to the cop shop and say sorry to the dirty, lucky bastard."

Rita Writes:
I have been to see Hugh Cooper again because I find him to be a fascinating character, and not just because he has promised to paint my portrait, though I am hoping that he will rub some of the Stormer's magic off on these wrinkled features. I doubt he can do much with the body and so I will forego divesting myself of clothing, no doubt to your eternal relief. You must realise that the photograph at the head of this column is several

years old and flatters me considerably. I currently look like the grandmother of the woman who appears above.

Anyway, to return to Hugh. Our meeting this time was not in the Dog's Breath but in a public park where Hugh is residing. Hugh claims that he is conducting an experiment in 'living on the edge' but I have my doubts. He had the hunted look of the husband who has been evicted by his wife, but Hugh plays his cards very close to his chest and would give nothing away about his personal life

The reason I'd tracked him down was to ask about the persistent rumours that have been circulating around parts of Glasgow that The Stormer is actually based on a real person and is not a figment of Hugh's imagination as he originally claimed. I told him that I tended to agree with him because The Stormer is inhumanly beautiful and any mortal cursed with such looks would carry a heavy burden indeed. I posited the notion that if not an exact likeness Hugh might have based the mural on someone he knew, and had exaggerated, but he denied this vehemently. The idea seemed to cause him so much distress that I immediately dropped that enquiry and asked instead of his future plans.

His answer was frank and disarming.

"I might give up painting," he said and when I expressed surprise he explained by saying, "I don't think I can top The Stormer. And if you can't aim high, what's the point?"

I insisted that a talent such as his should never be stifled after barely going through its birth pangs but he countered this by saying that far from being a birth, The Stormer was a culmination of his artistic career and I, for one, cannot deny that it is a tour de force and would be hard to surpass. However as one who feeds voraciously on The Stormer each time I pass it in the morning (and I take a long detour to achieve this), there was no way I was going to allow its creator to pack up his brushes.

I reminded him of his offer to paint my portrait and, ever a man of his word, he has agreed to make the attempt. If it meets with my approval, and with Hugh's hand on the brush I have no doubts, I shall plead with my editor to replace that pretty young thing above with something more becoming my years.

"Right, Shame," Hugh said, "You can't stay out here, it's going to be pissing down soon."

"Doesn't bother me."

"Aye, but it bothers me, I don't want you going down with double pneumonia."

Hugh tried to lift the tramp by his coat but Shame pushed him away. "I'm going nowhere, you have to be a regular wet weather warrior in this game, a wee bit of rain is nothing."

Hugh tried temptation. "I'm going for a curry."

"Can't. You're barred."

"I've found somewhere that's taken pity on me, an old pal of mine's invited me over."

"The man must be fearless. A restaurant could lose its license over one very edible cockroach. But I'm still not going with you. That lady has to be protected."

"She'll be alright for one night. Plus it's my birthday. You don't want me to eat alone on my birthday."

"You're just saying that. What birth sign are you?"

"I don't know, lesbian or thespian or something. Anyway, if you're my employee you're meant to do what you're told."

The Shame shrugged. "Where is this place?"

"Tandoori Palace, follow me."

They walked hurriedly towards the city centre and were soon ensconced in a fug of spices.

"Is the boss in?" Hugh asked the waiter as he seated them.

"You a health inspector?"

"Naww, tax man. Give Ganges a shout eh."

Hugh waved the menu away but the Shame studied it tentatively. "Like your bunnet, pal," he said to the waiter.

"Oh aye, turbans is great, 'cept when you've got an itchy heid."

The Shame stabbed a finger at the menu. "This dish here, this aloo saag, is it halal?"

The waiter kept a practiced straight face. "Oh aye, the tatties and the spinach are both ritually slaughtered."

The pair ordered and the waiter disappeared to pour the pre-prandial pints.

Ganges, thin enough to make you worry about his business, ghosted wearily from the kitchen and slumped down beside

Hugh. "I knew you would turn up, Hugh."

He stretched out his hand and Hugh shook it desperately. "No problems with my man here?" he asked gesturing to the Shame who looked out of place and uncomfortable.

"Not at all." He reached over and shook hands with the tramp. "We have undercover policemen who come in here who look worse than you. And they are cadging the free meals."

"Don't mention the police to me," Hugh said, "Anyway, how come you're serving me?"

"You are my friend."

Hugh shook his head. "My pals wouldn't piss on me if I was on fire these days. What makes you so keen to lose your food license?"

Ganges helped himself to Hugh's pakora. "A man should not be ruled by licenses."

Hugh pulled his plate closer. "What's your game, Ganges?"

Ganges smiled, revealing gold teeth. "You know me too well, Hugh my old friend. Let us just say that the Tandoori Palace is due to suffer a small accidental fire quite soon. We will definitely be serving the hottest curry in town that night."

"Business that bad?"

"The fashion is changing. They say that the Algerian sausage is coming. It will sweep all before it – the Macdonut, the Captain Sandra, the curry shops, the Chinese, the pizza, all gone." He paused to shout for another drink. "And I am bored with catering. I think I will become a bus driver again, it is much less complicated."

"You haven't driven a bus for twenty years, you'd never handle the traffic."

"Who cares? My insurance premium on the restaurant is fully paid up and I will gct a nice pay off. We will have a party after the fire."

Hugh polished off the last of his pakora and raised his glass to Ganges. "Well, I hope I live long enough to get an invite."

Ganges waved a finger at him. "You have been very naughty boy, Hugh. I would not be pleased if you painted my wife in her nakedness."

"Give us a break, Ganges, your missus must be about eighteen stone. I'd need to paint her on the side o' Ben Nevis. And I'd need Sherpa porters to carry the paint."

This thought seemed to intrigue Ganges, he disappeared into a reverie.

Their meals arrived and both Hugh and the Shame began demolishing them in good fashion, ladling the curry over the rice and going to work with their forks and scooping the sauce with torn off bits of naan bread.

On the last forkful Ganges came alive again. "You must not paint grafitti on my toilet wall, Hugh. I am scrub, scrub, scrubbing to get it off."

"It's no' grafitti, Ganges, it's folk art."

"It is a bloody mess. You wouldn't like it if I am writing Punjabi jokes on your toilet."

"What does it matter, you're burning the place down anyway."

Ganges grabbed his wrist. "Quietly please. It is not good to publicise these things."

The waiter collected their plates and returned to whisper in Ganges' ear. The thin Indian looked worried.

"Something wrong?" Hugh asked.

"Two waiters called off and this is due to be a busy night. Do you fancy a shift?"

"You've got to be kidding."

"Aye," Shame interjected, "It's his birthday, you can't expect him to graft on his birthday."

"Birthday?" Ganges snorted, "He is an artist, every day is a holiday to him. A good night's working will do him good."

Hugh looked shamefaced. "There's no need for honesty. Anyway, I don't know anything about working in an Indian restaurant."

"Why not? You have been doing the scoffing of my food for many years and you know the menu inside out."

"But I'm not Asian."

"So what? We'll say you're an albino or something."

"I'm not a waiter."

"You waited long enough to be a success. I'll pay you."

"I don't need money, I've still got the Stormer cash."

"Do me a favour."

Ganges had invited him to eat when others had rejected him, and Hugh knew that the impending fire had little to do with it.

He owed the little man.

"Deal," he said, sticking his hand out. "But just for tonight and I don't want wages, just keep the Shame topped up with lager."

"Not at all, I've got to get back to work," the tramp protested, but his heart wasn't in it. The thought of sitting in the rain depressed him despite everything he said.

Ganges stood up. "I don't know about that, I only pay the minimum wage and your friend here might be a demon drinker."

Hugh handed him a fifty pound note he peeled from the wad in his pocket. "Just keep the beer coming."

"So, you're paying me to work here? I like it. This is a marvellous new form of capitalism you've invented, Hugh. Do you want to be my partner?"

"That's desperate fast promotion," the Shame commented.

"Just a skill," Hugh smirked.

"Staff room and get changed," Ganges ordered.

"Aw no, I'm not wearing a monkey suit."

"You have to, you've got half your dinner down that t shirt."

"It's advertising. Punters can lick my shirt and see what they're going to get."

Ganges was stunned. "You are a genius, Hugh, just like that Rita woman in the *Herald* is saying. You have only been in the job five minutes and you've gone from being a waiter to being a partner to being the marketing director."

Hugh looked smug. "You wait till I get into the kitchen."

"Ah, you'll need to be careful there, they don't like innovation, Indian chefs. Their watchword is tradition. There are still some of them go out looking for cow pats in the morning to get the oven going."

Hugh noticed something. "You've lost your accent, Ganges."

Ganges did blush, but it didn't show through his tan. "You've rumbled me, Hugh. I only lose it with good friends, but I have to put it on for the punters, they expect it."

"Dear God, I've known you fifteen years."

"Aye, as a customer."

"Yeah, but you're Glasgow, and you've hidden it from me. Are you ashamed of it?"

Ganges put his hand on his shoulder, "Is it that important?"

"Of course it is."

"Glasgow, lived here most of my life. It's really the only home I know. What do you say about our city?"

There were a million mawkish thoughts in Hugh's head, and all were ultimately boring and embarrassing. What did he have to say about his city ? He loved it, he hated it, he'd fight for it. But would he die for it?

And what made it?

The people? The buildings? The streets? The parks?

"Well, for a start, you'll never find your average man-in-the-street in Glasgow. Everyone's a minted character. There's no John Does, not one Joe Bloggs; just one man mobs, wild eyed immortals, kings o' the castle. There's a little madness in Glasgow. And it's great."

"I know that," Ganges agreed.

"Naww, what you're thinking about is drunks, and gangs, and football hooligans. All the pish the media feed you. That's not the madness I mean."

For some reason Ganges adopted his Indian persona again. "Why do you say this? I know the madness you are talking of. I can reach out and touch it, I am not blind."

Hugh's first self-imposed commandment had always been not to make assumptions about people, and he just had.

"I'm sorry, Ganges," he said, "I'm talking down to you, and you're as Glasgow as me. You see, Glasgow exists. It's not vague, like Scotland. Scotland isn't a nation, it's a notion. And some people are going off the notion."

"Really?" and the Glaswegian Ganges was back, "I'd taken you for a Scotsman as well as a Glaswegian."

"Oh, I'm Scots and proud of it, but I've got more in common with you than a crofter from South Uist."

Ganges pulled his new employee to his feet and embraced him. "Get dressed and get to work."

Hugh knew a lot of people in the drama business - actors, directors, writers - and they'd often encouraged him to take a greater interest, but he didn't think he breathed the same air as them. There wasn't the compulsion.

His contribution to drama had been limited to drawing posters for plays and the designing and building of the famous, giant, papier-mache, vibrator. But, like most people, Hugh was a natural actor. He slipped into roles constantly on his voyage through life. To some people he was artist, to some wit, to others half-wit, and all unconsciously, without the dread accusation of *acting*.

It was time. The pubs were spewing out their drunks, all eager to mate German beer with curried chicken, and look forlorn at the technicolour results. Hugh handled them with wit, poise, charm, and downright cheek. It was hard work, but he enjoyed it. There was the social contact, abusive though some of it was. There was sheer pain from his feet, unused to standing, unused to carrying plates, dishes, trays.

He loved the clatter of the kitchen, the verbal fencing with the chefs when he mispronounced a dish. The controlled aggression of telling a drunk to pay up and get out. Somewhere after two, when he had a chance of a quick breather, he noticed that table seventeen, which he had been serving, held four good-looking women. They were down to their coffee, and he'd only just noticed them. Had he been that busy?

He was sneaking a quick restorative vodka behind the bar when he saw in the mirror that one of them was looking towards him. It wasn't the look of a woman summoning a waiter. And he was knackered.

He swallowed the last of the vodka and handed the empty glass to Ganges. "I'm out of here," he whispered from the side of his mouth.

"Not going to enjoy the fringe benefits?" Ganges asked.

"Not tonight, I'm wasted. But I'm a natural, Ganges, born to be an Indian waiter. Three plates, each hand, no problem. But the next time I do this gig I'm not doing it half-arsed with just a monkey suit. I want a turban."

"I'll order one for you, extra large is it?"

5. VANDALISM

Crawford sat in the van he'd had to hire to transport the paint and ladders and cursed the expenditure. As he'd guessed, the whole thing had spiralled out of control. What he'd imagined to be simplicity itself, getting a couple of neds to vandalise the painting, was turning into an operation with the complexity of

D Day. He peered through the drizzle trying to catch sight of Slab and his gang but saw nothing but Saturday night revellers staggering down the street. That had been another of his miscalculations. For him, midnight was late, whereas half the city seemed to be still out on the lash and the anonymity Crawford required just wasn't there. A police car drove by and Crawford hid his face.

A couple of lads in the mandatory hooded tops stood at the street corner. Were they Slab's cohorts? Crawford knew he was taking a chance with Slab. His little gang were a small-time operation with delusions of grandeur, but were just the types to commit acts of random vandalism. Crawford only prayed that they would stand by their word and wouldn't confess his complicity in the whole affair. It was a chance he had to take.

Yes, that was Slab, unmistakably towering over his companions. But it was still too early, there were too many people about. Crawford was damned if he was going to go and stand in the rain with them, he pumped his horn impatiently.

After a while Slab realised this message was intended for him and ambled over to the van and climbed into the passenger seat. The van's springs creaked in complaint.

Slab beamed a wide smile. "Hullo, boss. The boys are all here. You got the stuff?"

"In the back," Crawford said. "But it's too early, there are still too many people around."

"Clubs," Slab replied, "People out dancing, on the pull, looking for nooky. Dirty buggers. They'll be off soon, couple of hours maybe."

"Will that leave you enough time to get the job done? It starts getting light about eight and you need to be well gone by then."

Slab cast a professional eye up at the wall. "You just want it messed up?"

"Precisely."

Slab nodded and his double chins jiggled. "Yeah, we can do that."

Crawford cleared his throat. "I won't be able to return to pick up the ladders, so you can keep them. But I don't want you using them in any criminal enterprises. Breaking and entering, that sort of thing. You have to promise me that."

Slab nodded. "Domestic use only, I get it, Mr Gillespie. You have my word on it."

"Yes, use them to decorate your houses, not break into factories."

"We don't do factories no more, Mr Gillespie, just offices. It's more upmarket like."

"Yes, of course, can't fault your ambition."

Now it was Slab's turn to clear his throat. "This rain, boss, that's an unexpected factor."

"So your boys might get a little wet, I'm sure you've worked in worse conditions."

Slab was affronted. "Oh, it's not that, boss, my boys is fearless, little rain won't bother them. Thing is, it's a matter of health and safety."

"Health and safety?"

"The rain falls, The ground gets wet, the ladders slip, and poor old Slab ends up with a broken leg. And let's face it, you haven't got any employer's liability insurance for us, have you?"

Crawford had to admit that this was true. "How much?" he asked.

"Boys reckon a twenty pound wet weather bonus should cover it."

Crawford had spent so much he didn't care any more. "Certainly. And you'll probably get peckish in the middle of the night. Shall I arrange a food delivery for you"

Slab gave a big rumbling laugh. "No need, boss, Charlie brought sandwiches."

They sat in silence for a while and the rain eased and the streets started to clear. Eventually Slab eased his huge bulk from the seat. "I'll get the boys ready," he promised. Crawford cheered inwardly, he was tired, it was well past his bedtime and the further he was from here when the deed was done, the better."

He patted the big man's broad back. "Good luck."

Slab wandered over and joined his unkempt troop.

The smallest member of the gang, Malky, was unhappy. "I don't trust that bastard," he said. "He'll stitch us up. He's the kind of bastard that would fit you up with drunk and disorderly, breach of the peace, an' keeping a goat up a close without a license."

"No, no," Slab placated, "Mr Gillespie's sound. He'll no'let us down."

It didn't work. "You watch," the little ned said, "the minute we start throwing paint at that wall he'll come over and lift us."

"Relax, we've got his money."

"Aye, but he's devious. He's up to something."

They stood shivering as the darkness deepened. Almost as if hypnotised they turned as one and stared up at the painting. It was if it had been painted with fluorescent paint; despite the gloom and covered in rain The Stormer not only glistened but glowed. Slab and company were transfixed.

"That should be in the art galleries," Malky whispered.

"Aye," Doug agreed, "that's beautiful, that is. What's he got against it anyway?"

"None of our business," Slab said. "He wants a job done and we're the boys to do it."

They continued to stand and stare and Crawford watching them drummed his fingers impatiently on the steering wheel. He'd decided that the minute they'd unloaded the ladders and paint he'd drive off and return in ten minutes to ensure they were getting on with it before heading home. But they weren't even moving and the streets were almost empty. It was too late to pump his horn at them again, he'd be drawing attention to himself. He swung his cramped legs out from the van and despite their protests, walked over to the gang.

"Come on, lads, time to get a move on."

"Oh aye, boss, no bother." Slab herded his troop to the back of the van and they unloaded the equipment in silence. The minute they were done Crawford slid back into the driver's seat and sped off. With reluctant energy the gang moved the stuff from the kerb to the wall.

Ten minutes later, when Crawford returned they were sitting on the paint pots and smoking. Crawford, furious, dashed over to them.

"What are you playing at?"

"It's the ladders, Mr Gillespie," Slab explained, "They're not long enough. They're domestic and we need commercial, either that or scaffolding. We can hardly reach the bottom of the painting."

It was yet another unforeseen problem and required Crawford's skill in crisis management.

"Poles," Crawford said.

"Poles?"

"Stick your brushes on poles and you'll be able to reach."

Slab considered this. "Okay, you get poles and we'll come back tomorrow night."

The last thing Crawford wanted was another night like this.

"So you don't have any poles?"

"We like to travel light."

Crawford nodded and realised that the drizzle was increasing. His brain only really worked at maximum efficiency in a crisis. Now he was masterful and decisive.

"There is a box of latex gloves among the items I purchased. I'd thought they could help to eliminate evidence in the form of fingerprints, but they can serve another purpose. You will fill these gloves with the paint. You will then run across this grassed area and hurl the gloves at the painting, thus spattering it with Precious Pink . This will also help in making this look like an act of random vandalism as opposed to my original concept of painting over the entire area. Concentrate on the face and the naughty bits."

With that he about-turned and marched back to the van. Slab and his troop slowly got to work, unpacking the gloves and opening the cans of paint. Crawford watched, satisfied that things were moving forward well.

But as Slab and his gang stood with gloves full of paint at the edge of the grassed area they hesitated. Once again they were driven to stare at that which they were being asked to survive.

"Are you greeting, big man?" Malky asked.

"Am I fuck. It's this rain."

"It's a crime," Malky said.

"No," Slab argued, "it's a sin."

"I can't do it," Doug complained.

"Me neither. But it's a lot of money to lose."

"We should stick to what we know. Bit of robbing, good dishonest work. Christmas is coming, time of opportunity."

They stared up at her and The Stormer spoke to them.

They walked en-masse over to the van and Slab rapped on the window. Crawford wound it down with a puzzled look on his face.

"We're villains, Mr Gillespie," Slab explained, "We don't deny it. We'll rob, we'll hurt, we'll cause chaos. But what you're proposing is uncivilised and we don't do uncivilised."

He thrust Crawford's money into his lap and the gang turned and walked slowly away.

The next day a Triumph Bonneville with extended forks and ape-hanger handle bars puttered up to the site of the mural and the rider kicked down the stand and dismounted with fluidity and style. Midden walked over to Shame and gave him a hard stare.

"You Shame?"

"That is I," the tramp replied.

Midden handed over a twenty pound note and said, "Hugh sent that for you."

"A bonus? When I almost failed him. There were paint pots and ladders lying here when we came back last night."

"Not your fault, Hugh reckons."

Shame disappeared the note and said, "He is a prince amongst men, our Hugh. And you are?"

"Just a pal. Name's Midden."

"Nice one. Would suit me. Fancy a swap?"

"No thanks, it's an heirloom."

"I like your motoring cycle. It's very nice. I used to have a motoring cycle once, many, many years ago, when I lived among you mortals. A Honda Fifty."

"Aye, that was a long time ago."

"It served me to get to work."

"Oh aye, what did you work at?"

"I was a progress chaser. Problem was, I could never catch it."

"Know what you mean."

Midden produced a packet of cigarettes and gave one to the Shame.

"How is our artistic genius?" Shame asked.

"He's fine. Laying low."

"He's a clever boy. That painting's a belter."

"He's done better."

"No, I can't believe that."

"Straight up. Well, to my mind anyway. You've got to remember, Hugh's been painting all his life, done hundreds of them. This one's just getting all the publicity because it's so fucking big. If that was on a four foot by two foot canvas nobody would ever have heard of it."

Shame sucked deeply on the cigarette. "I'd imagined this was his masterwork."

"Naah, far from it. He captures movement very well for one thing and The Stormer's just lying there. He just got lucky with this one. And he was due it."

"It might be luck but to my mind that's a brilliant piece of art."

"Doesn't matter how good you are, you need luck. But Hugh's good, painted the tank on my bike. Come and have a look."

They strolled over to Midden's chopper and the Shame was suitably impressed. "Yes, indeed, our boy can paint. But he must surely have had some success before this."

"Dribs and drabs, he'd tell you himself. But he needed a big breakthrough piece and I think he's finally got it."

"Oh aye, nobody could deny him now, not after Her."

"You'd be surprised, some fuckwit'll turn round and say it was a fluke. Or it's only impressive because of its size or location. To be a genuine success he'll need to keep hammering them with greatness or they'll forget him."

There was a doubt in Midden's words which the Shame caught. "Do you think he can't do it?"

"Listen, Shame, our Hugh Cooper is his own worst enemy. He's a rebel and a renegade and won't conform to any rules you throw at him. He needed everybody to know how good he was and he fought like fuck for it for years. Kicked in the balls every now and again, but kept going. You've got to admire his guts, 'cause a lot of the guys he trained with went and started doing layouts in newspapers, just to make a living. Not Hugh, he wouldn't lie down. But it's just as likely that now he's achieved this he'll throw it all in and become a plumber, just to be awkward."

"I can't believe that."

"You don't know Cooper."

The Shame stubbed out his cigarette and looked about him. "Listen, don't let me keep you."

"Don't worry, I'm on wages to be here."

The Shame looked worried. "Is there something brewing?"

"No, no, just Hugh reckoned you could do with some company for a while. It must be boring standing about here all day."

"Far from it. It's a joy just watching people's faces when they see The Stormer. Look around you."

Midden scanned the people who were walking past, hesitating, looking, smiling, and he smiled too. "Jeeze, you're right."

"You can' get bored seeing other people happy."

"And he pays you for this? You're in clover, my man."

"Beats chasing progress."

Midden seemed embarrassed about asking the question. "C'mon, how did you end up in this state? You seem like an intelligent guy."

The Shame grinned. "Pissed off with the world. Not brave enough for suicide. Just let everything go. It's easy."

"Well I'm no pillar of society, but I'd never let myself fall that low. No offence."

"None taken, Midden. But it takes all sorts, and maybe I'm just taking a wee break from the rat-race and I'll be back some day. I tend not to plan ahead."

"If you're ever stuck, me and the boys drink down in the Dog's Breath. There'll always be somebody there can bail you out."

"Oh aye, what's the password?"

Midden smiled. "Take a guess."

The Shame followed Midden's gaze up to the wall and matched his smile. "Oh aye, I know."

Back in middle class land Audrey and several other housewives were perched around Davina's lounge whispering urgently. As Davina entered, carrying coffee and cakes on a tray, the others all pulled out mural clippings from the

newspaper and waved them at her while singing to the tune of
'She'll Be Coming Round The Mountain',
"If your tits are in the tabloids, you're a tart !
If your tits are in the tabloids, you're a tart !"
Davina laughed and kicked out at the obvious instigator, her
dear, dear friend, Audrey.

6. PEACE TALKS?

Crawford was busy at his desk, thumbing through paperwork
when Sergeant Watt came to the door with Hugh just behind
him.
"A Mr Cooper for you, sir," Watt said.
Crawford looked up and smiled falsely. "Ahh, our local
Michelangelo. Come in, take a pew. What can I do for you, as
if I didn't know?"
Hugh hesitated, unsure of Crawford's mood, but then took a
seat opposite him at the desk.
"I don't want any trouble."
Crawford continued fiddling about with his paperwork, trying
to show his lack of interest. "Trouble? Trouble? Don't know
what you mean.   I'm a policeman, it's my job to prevent
trouble."
"Call the dogs off," Hugh said flatly.
"Dogs ? Are the canine branch involved?"
"Don't take the piss," Hugh complained.
Now Crawford gave Hugh his full attention. "Hah, you don't
like it when you're the victim, do you?   It's okay when you're
shovelling on the insolence, but when the boot's on the other
foot, then you're crying police brutality."
Hugh was confused at Crawford's little rant. He looked down
at Crawford's scratch-pad which was covered in doodles,
cartoon nudes in the pose of The Stormer. "Are you all right ?"
Crawford quickly moved his arm to cover up the doodles.
"Perfectly."
"Look, it was only a tribute ... to my first love. You can paint
one too ... a self-portrait. I haven't seen Davina for over ten
years."
"So you just imagined what she looked like naked?"
So that's what was tearing the poor bastard's insides.

Cuckolded by a paintbrush. "No, Crawford, I've got an old photo of Davina lying on Ayr beach. Wearing a bikini. I painted out the bikini and changed the background, that's all."

Crawford's hand twitched. "Well .... you've captured her ... bodily parts .. perfectly."

Hugh smiled. "Oh, thanks very much. That's very kind of you."

"It wasn't meant as a compliment, you little shit. And I don't credit you with that good an imagination."

"That was always your lack, wasn't it Crawford, no imagination." Hugh snarled it out, but suddenly felt sorry for the poor, demented man. "Listen, I've never seen Davina McLean with no clothes on, that's a fact. Not that I'd be averse to it."

"You're a liar ... with a sewer of a mind."

They were like knights in heavy armour who could only fight in short bursts, before retreating to draw breath and lick their wounds.

"What do you want?" Hugh asked. "What do I have to do? Do you want to give me a kicking, is that it?"

Crawford smiled, an ugly thing. "A kicking? Oh no, no, a bloody nose is the least you can look forward to, man. You seem to be under the impression, Cooper, that you have some claim on this city, but as I've told you, I have power here, this is my city."

"No, Crawford," Hugh breathed, "Glasgow belongs to me."

"Hah, easily said. And speaking of bloody noses I've heard that the Special Operations Unit have taken a dislike to you."

Hugh winced. "The Mad Skwad? That's going a bit nuclear is it no'? It's not like I'm some big drugs dealer or a mass murderer."

Crawford was in his element. "The S.O.U. like to keep their hand in. We have to wring some genuine remorse out of you. I actually thought you'd have lasted out longer."

"I'm not here for me," Hugh explained. "I've got a relationship of my own I'm trying to save."

Crawford patted a thick file that lay in his 'Pending' tray. "Ah now, I've been checking up on you, this'll be your prostitute friend."

58

"She's not a tart!"

"Oh, what do you prefer ?   A strumpet, a slut, harlot, trollop, bimbo, good-time-that's-been-had-by-all .....?"

Hugh smiled weekly, he'd heard it all before and now Crawford was laid bare before him.

"Leave it out, sad-case.   What do you want?"

"I want that painting gone."

"Can't be done."

Crawford started flicking through the file and held a photograph of Fiona up to the light.

Hugh saw his chance. "But I could change it.   What if I stuck a swim-suit on her, then nobody would be able to see your wife's lovely, luscious body ?"   He watched his foe to gauge his reactions then continued. "Hide away her secret charms, her intimate parts.   Would that do?   Or I could paint hair on her chest.   Or a moustache?   I get the feeling you'd like a wife with a moustache."

Crawford came flying across the desk with a roar but Hugh had been waiting for him.   He moved aside so that Crawford crashed to the floor, with files and other office debris falling on top of him.

The noise brought Watt and other officers rushing to the door. They found Hugh sitting unperturbed and Crawford in a pile on the floor. Hugh shrugged and stood up. As he passed the doorway observers he looked back at the groaning Crawford and said dismissively, "He fell."   It was a line he thought policemen would understand.

But the Mad Skwad worried him. They didn't take prisoners.

Glasgow was once a city of ants.

Glasgow, twenty three miles from the open sea and sitting on a river that was once no more than a trout stream.   But Glasgow made the Clyde and the Clyde made Glasgow."

That city was gone.   Where were the twelve and a half miles of quays and docks on the river?   Where were the quarter of the world's tonnage the city once built?   Where were the 2,000 separate industries it held in 1960?"

An alien observer, sitting on high, would once have seen a dark hive of industry.   Hooters blowing, black streams of smoke, hunched men in their thousands going to work iron, build ships, create engines, belch fire. And there was always a darkness, always a dread shuddering of the ants, unsure as to their purpose, frightened by their fate.

To dispel the fear, it seemed, they made noise. A great surging rush. As if they had some imperative for a great destiny, that they would see the lands they built their engines to dominate. And feel the sun on their face.

That was all gone now.

But Glasgow was still a talking city, it retained that much of its past. It had not gone cold with the removal of its layers of grime and darkness.

Hugh was sure there was some mafia of old wifies who formed the backbone of this grapevine. Once, at seventeen, he'd lumbered a girl at the dancing and taken her back to her house in Whiteinch. It had been a cold night and, amongst the dustbins, when Hugh produced his white inch, the girl screamed. There was a bit of a commotion and Hugh fled to the safety of the 64 bus. When he got home his mother belted him for being a dirty pig.

How had she known? They weren't even on the phone then.

Glasgow talked.

And now it talked of The Stormer. It talked of Crawford Gillespie and the Mad Skwad. It talked of Hugh Cooper ... and his impending doom.

Rita Writes:

The plot thickens! You will recall that I have taken more than a passing interest in the fabulous mural The Stormer and its creator, Hugh Cooper. I learned recently that it seems to be common knowledge that the painting bears more than a passing resemblance to the wife of a senior police officer. As Hugh has been visiting me in the course of painting my portrait I took the opportunity to ask about this similarity, despite his previous claims that he had created The Stormer from his own imagination. Finally, after much wheedling on my part, he admitted that he had known the said policeman's wife when she was a schoolgirl and that he had been attracted to her. She was, in essence, his first love. So, when it came to painting the most beautiful woman he could imagine, he had drawn on this long lost memory to give The Stormer substance. This, I hope, will stop the trollops who have been infesting the bars and clubs of Glasgow and claiming that they were the inspiration. Having long legs and red hair does not give them the right to claim immortality.

This lady, who Hugh will not name, is happily married and has no problems with the painting, according to Hugh. Whoever she is, she is one lucky lady. Not the Mona Lisa or Helen of Troy have been displayed to such perfection. A combination, I think, of a perfect beauty and a master artist.

Hugh is having less joy with yours truly, he may be the master artist, but as the perfect beauty I fail miserably.

Davina was serious about her jogging and wore skin tight leggings and t-shirt with her designer trainers. She also alternated gentle running with passionate sprints and often attracted the attention of men who could admire a fit young woman loping along at a goodly pace. Today, in a park slowly turning Autumn, she was joined by a scruffy, ill-dressed character who struggled to run alongside her. Davina barely looked at him.

Staring straight ahead, but speaking loudly enough so that he would hear, she said, "If you don't bugger off, I'll call the police."

"There's no law against jogging," came the reply.

She glanced over at him. "In a trench coat and cowboy boots?"

"It's advanced jogging, Davey," a vaguely familiar voice said.

She began to slow down, looked over at him again, and eased down till she came to a stop. She stared at him.

"Nobody's called me Davey for almost twenty years. And there was only one guy then."

Hugh bowed. "I have returned. Sorry about the delay."

She grinned and looked at the man, "The moustache is new, but there's only one Hugh Cooper. God's gift to insanity. You haven't changed. From dirty drawings on a school lavvy wall to gable ends."

Hugh grinned back, pleased that he hadn't been rebuffed. "Yeah, that's me. Have you seen it? Do you like it?"

"What's not to like. It's me, a bit idealised, but me."

"Well, from what I could remember. I had a faded Polaroid from a school bus trip to the coast."

Davina took a deep breath. "It's a great painting, Hugh, but you should have asked me."

Hugh nodded in agreement. "I am here to apologise, to say sorry, to beg your forgiveness ... and to ask you to get that nutter of a husband of yours off my back."

Davina saw the genuine worry on his face and was moved. "Mmm, he's not taken it well, but I don't think I can do anything about that."

Hugh's face dropped even further.

"All my friends think I posed for you" Davina continued, "That I'm some kind of femme fatale. It's been quite fun."

Hugh searched for more sympathy but couldn't find the right words. "It was all a long time ago. Kids trying to find themselves. Time passes, but some things you don't forget."

She suppressed a sniff and said, "Oh Hugh. You never really asked, did you, never really pushed it."

"You were playing a safe game, Davey. You wanted security, a police cadet, not an art student."

"Not true. You treated me too much like a Stormer, and too little like a human being."

The memories came flooding back to her and she revelled in their embrace. "And I wanted a gentleman, not an octopus."

"I couldn't help my hormones."

She smiled at the thought of Hugh's dangerous wandering hands and the art that had emerged from them. The conversation seemed to be going nowhere and she reverted to type. "Are you.. have you .. been ...married?"

And Hugh, as he had to, reverted to his own type. "Naah, lived with a guy for four years, but we split up. He wanted kids and I'd had a vasectomy."

She grinned again and its brightness drowned the damply emerging sun. "God, I was so stupid. You always used to cover up with some goofy line."

She suddenly held out her hand. "Hullo, Hugh, it's good to see you again. I've missed you."

Hugh took her hand in both of his. "You should have phoned. I was in."

She laughed and slipped her arm through his as they started walking, but she was holding him at a distance, she sensed the octopus was only sleeping.

At our gable end wall the same constables who had been tasked with placing cones were removing them from the street and cursing their superior. An open-top tour bus was driving past, tourists excitedly taking photographs of The Stormer.

Sitting on one of the benches in the landscaped area was Shame, being unobtrusive by reading a Chinese newspaper. He eyed the tourists warily and made notes in his notebook. He took a swig from a bottle of cheap wine before turning again to his newspaper. His attention was so concentrated that, for a moment, it seemed that he could actually read it.

In the massage parlour Midden was making a plea to his sister on behalf of his friend. Fiona listened absent-mindedly while massaging another punter and really taking out all her fury on him.

"He says he didn't paint you in the buff because he respects you," Midden explained, "Can you handle that?"

Fiona pouted. "We've been together three years, Midden. It's not as if he doesn't know what I look like naked."

Midden wondered why she was sharing this confidence. "Are you listening to what I'm telling you?"

Fiona slapped her customer's arse soundly, leaving a distinctive hand print. "What about the red-head then?"

"First thing that came into his head. You know Hugh."

Fiona softened, her pummelling of the punter became less severe. He looked disappointed. "Okay, I'll talk to him," Fiona conceded, "But he'll need to get down on his knees and apologise."

Midden nodded and headed for the door but turned suddenly to lower his face into the punter's. "That's my sister," he said, "so you watch yourself. Try anything on and I'll come round to your house .... and *not* give you a good belting."

The punter looked even more disappointed.

Rita Writes:

My portrait is nearly finished and I hope to have it atop this column within the next few weeks. Hugh has admitted defeat in his attempt to make me look beautiful and has settled for a handsome dignity. The effect is actually quite startling. He has somehow managed to make me look as if I am curious, and curiosity is the leitmotif of the journalist. Is this Hugh Cooper's special skill? That he can identify the inner working of our souls and embody them in oils. If so, it is a special gift, and lengthy tomes have been written and biopics made in an effort to relate what Hugh captures with a few quick strokes of his brush.

It is time the arts establishment woke up to this supremely talented young man and gave him better things to do than painting withered old hackettes. Because of a personal misfortune he has no back catalogue to exhibit and so the only way we can enjoy more of that Cooper magic is by commissioning him. Come on, ladies, who doesn't want to be painted by the man who painted The Stormer? My portrait was originally Hugh's idea and he believes that this removes any onus on me to reward him for his effort. He is mistaken.

"What's new, sweetheart?" Audrey, the bad influence, was at the door with a litre of Chardonnay and a bad Bogey impression. Davina ushered her in and fetched glasses.

"I saw him. Hugh. The artist."

Audrey smiled knowingly and sipped at her wine. "Discuss the finer points of your anatomy, did you?"

"You're sick. Hugh wanted me to get Crawford to stop harassing him."

Audrey held on to the smile. "Didn't want a bit of nooky or anything then?"

"What is wrong with you? Is that all you think about? You're obsessed!"

Audrey put down her glass and lit a cigarette. "I have seen that painting, dear girl, and it was done by a man who desperately wants to shag you."

Davina had the grace to blush. "He may well want to .. but that doesn't mean .."

"What?" Audrey cooed, "Is diddums going to knock back the nasty little man when he comes pawing round her underwear?"

Davina tilted her head back a little, searching for an air of authority. "You must have a very unhappy sex life, Audrey, to be so interested in mine."

"I don't have a sex life, Davina. I have Tom, my beloved husband, and three children. I'm only trying to get a little vicarious excitement through your shenanigans."

"But I'm not doing anything!"

Audrey exhaled smoke violently but happily, "Not yet, but the build-up's the best bit!"

"There is no build-up. Because nothing's going to happen. I didn't invest all these years in being Mrs Crawford Gillespie for nothing."

They sat silently for a while, old friends, reading each other's minds.

"Are you happy?" Audrey finally asked.

"What kind of stupid question is that?"

"The kind that rarely gets a yes-no answer."

Again silence. Davina poured more wine and put on some music. Eventually, having run out of things she could do to avoid the issue she sat down again, closer to Audrey this time.

"It's true, I've been feeling unfulfilled. I've been re-evaluating my life. And yes, this painting has brought a bit of excitement into my life .. and I'm enjoying the attention .."

Audrey grabbed her friend's arm gleefully. "Yes! Yes! And now you're going to let the wee painter shag you!"

Davina finally decided to join Audrey's mood. "God no! I'm looking for truckers, brickies .. a *real* bit of rough."

Back at the garage Midden crowed about his achievement. "Good news, Hugh. I've done the job. She's willing to talk to you."

Hugh nodded impassively, took a wad of notes from his pocket and peeled off some cash which he passed to Midden. "Well done. Tell her I'll pick up the rest of my stuff next week."

Midden thrust the cash into a pocket of his greasy denims and tried to elaborate. "No, she's up for peace talks. I've earned my crust, healed the breach. I should get a job with the United Nations. “

Hugh wasn't listening. “It's over, Midden, there's no point in kidding on.”

“Oh shit !   I spun her a brilliant line too.”

“I went to see her,” Hugh explained, “Davina.”

Midden could see what was coming and looked horrified. “Her you painted?   Bad move, Hugh boy.   Not recommended. Danger!   Danger!” Hugh's lack of response worried him. “Shit! Shit! Shit!   The Feef will absolutely murder you.”

7. FOOD & DRINK

Back at the mural the Shame was marching up and down in front of the mural in a very business-like guardsman fashion when Hugh approached him.

“I hope you're not checking up on me,” the Shame said, “I don't take kindly to management harassment.”

Hugh placated him with more money. “Not at all, you're doing a great job. Why don't you nip down to the chippie and get us something to eat.”

The Shame pushed the money away. “You don't catch me out that way. No eating on duty.”

“No, seriously, get me a smoked sausage supper and whatever you want for yourself.”

But the Shame was not so easily swayed, “No no, deserting my post, can't do that.”

“Shame! I'm starving!” Hugh said desperately, “Please get me something to eat.”

Realisation dawned on The Shame. “Oh, so you're still ....”

“Aye! Barred! Plus, that half wit's got the Mad Skwad after me. And though it shows the decline in my culinary standards, in two minutes I'm going to eat you. After giving you a wash, of course.”

The Shame started back. “There's no need for cannibalism!”

He took Hugh's money and asked, “I don't suppose you've had any luck finding somewhere to stay either?”

Hugh shook his head. “It's Hughie no pals time. You'd be surprised, guys you've known for years, thought you could trust, all of a sudden they've got partners that don't want to get involved, or landlords that won't approve, or some such shit."

"Hugh, my boy," the Shame said, "I am one of life's survivors, and there are certain survival skills I think I must teach you." He put an arm around Hugh.

"Thanks, Shame."

"Being your accommodation and sustenance officer, as well as my guard duties will, of course, entail further expenditure on your part, but let us discuss the precise details over the aforesaid smoked sausage supper. Pickled onion?"

At the large Olympic sized swimming pool in the newly modernised sports centre Davina and Audrey were treading water while, down at the shallow end, some of their friends were marshalling a bunch of their kids. Audrey was in a revealing bikini, but Davina's costume would cause the Pope no qualms.

Davina tried to explain something to her friend. "It was good to see him again, that's all. We chatted, he makes me laugh."

But Audrey was wise. "It's a recipe for disaster, a guy that's carried a torch for you for twenty years turns up again." But then she confessed. "I admit it, I'm jealous."

Davina splashed water at her. "It's not like that, we went our separate ways long ago. There was never that much between us and there's nothing between us now, and neither one of us wants there to be."

Audrey made a disbelieving face.

Up in the viewing gallery Hugh appeared and waved down at them. Davina was hugely embarrassed but Audrey stared right back and asked, "Is that him? Is that your artist guy? He doesn't look like much, very much a mini Cooper"

"Yeah, he was never a giant," Davina admitted, "but he's a nice guy."

Audrey scrutinised him more closely. "Uh huh. Is the scruffiness mandatory in a bit of rough?"

Gibson and Robb, two plain-clothes CID men were lounging about in their office, drinking coffee and reading magazines. Or rather, studying the evidence they'd obtained in a porn bust.

Crawford entered and the two rose to their feet lazily and obviously unimpressed by him.

"Morning, lads," Crawford said jauntily.

The response carried less enthusiasm.

Crawford waved them back to their seats and perched on the edge of a desk. "Keeping busy?"

"Snowed under, sir," Robb said, "Kidnapping, robbery, hijacks, murder, mayhem, it's all go. How about things in the community involvement branch?"

"Oh, we have our moments," Crawford said.

"I saw you mentioned in the paper last week, sir. Anti-smoking in the car, wasn't it? Don't Draw and Drive, that was it."

He took a long draught of his coffee.

Crawford didn't recognise the sarcasm. "Absolutely, very easy to lose concentration."

"So what can we do for you, sir?" Gibson said, "School kids needing lectured to again?"

"No no, I have my own men on that. No, I was wondering how you lads were on prostitution?"

"Quite partial to it myself, sir," Robb said.

Gibson fired him a dirty look as Crawford looked uncomfortable.

"Oh, a joke," Crawford said finally, "I see. Ha ha, very good. No, there's this girl I want seeing to."

"Oh yeah?"

"She needs to be taken care off."

Robb nudged Gibson.

"Oh, bit of a picture, is she?"

Crawford glared at them, but they feigned innocence.

"No, bad sort. Call-girl, prostitute, that sort of thing. Works in a massage parlour. I think she should be arrested."

Gibson shook his head. "We tend to leave the working girls alone, sir, especially if they're operating from a sauna and not being a nuisance on the streets."

"But she's an affront to decency, man. A trollop, a bimbo, a strumpet. Fornicating outwith the marital bed, for money, passing on social diseases, decaying the moral fabric of our society."

68

Gibson swallowed the last of his coffee. "Is this official then, sir?"

"Well ... not .. precisely."

"Ah, if you could make it official, sir, we'd be more than happy to arrest your friend. But, as it is, maybe the best bet is for you to go and give her a damn good arresting yourself."

Crawford slid off the desk and straightened himself up. "Yes, yes, perhaps you're right. No need to bother you lads." He smiled at them with a forced cheeriness and left.

The two CID men turned to look at each other and both mouthed one word …wanker!

Rita Writes:

The image you see above is a poor representation of what Mr Hugh Cooper has created with only my own poor visage for inspiration. The digital arts cannot yet capture in pixels what Hugh has done. He has called it Rita The Writer and it is, I suppose, the only legacy I shall leave apart from the scribblings I have assailed you with for the last thirty years. This is a painting that I will bequeath to my children and grandchildren with pride. It currently hangs proudly in my lounge and two year old Alice, my daughter's youngest, though used to my appearances in the paper and on television, still reckons that Nana looks better on the wall than in reality.

I spoke to the Lady Provost recently and she told me that she will soon be commissioning her own portrait from Hugh to hang in the City Chambers. She is very impressed with The Stormer and is practicing languorous poses in preparation.

Is success finally going to shine on Hugh Cooper? Will The Stormer be more than a one-hit wonder? I anticipate the day when Hugh attacks Edinburgh and London and New York, paint brush in hand and with an indomitable spirit. The dolly birds of Hollywood would do well to have themselves immortalised by this man who does in paint what Robert Burns did in verse. No-one deserves the fanfare more. In the immortal words of our city, "Gaun yersel, wee man!"

Outside the sports centre Davina and her friends with their kids all come out together. The kids were running about and being chased by their mothers. Hugh was standing near the exit but didn't approach them. Audrey spotted him first.

In as loud a voice as she could manage she bellowed. "Better get home, Davina, your *husband* will be expecting his dinner."

Davina followed her gaze and saw Hugh. She hurriedly passed her sports bag to Audrey and ran her fingers through her still-wet hair. "Just a chat," she explained to the blonde.

"I've never heard it called chatting before, but make sure he gives you a bloody good chat."

Davina gave her a playful shove and walked over to Hugh. "Hi."

"Hi, Davey. I felt like a bloody pervert watching you lot down there. I must do it more often."

"I thought maybe you were checking to see how accurate you'd got your picture."

"Don't need to, I've got an artistic license from the Arts Council."

She started leading him towards the car-park. "Can I give you a lift?"

"You already have

"Ooh, flattery, I like it," she simpered

But Hugh wasn't really in the mood. "You have to talk to Crawford, he's making my life a misery."

But Davina was having too much fun. "Didn't your mother teach you anything, you don't paint policemen's wives in the nude."

Hugh raised his voice a little to jolt her out of her merriment. "This isn't funny, Davey. What he's doing is illegal. You can't hound a man out of town in this day and age. This isn't the Wild West. If I have to go to a lawyer to get this sorted out, your Crawford could lose his job. End of career, end of prospects, all your efforts gone for nothing."

Davina sensed his anguish and went cold. "He won't listen to me, Hugh. He never has. But if I stand up for you, it'll only make him more paranoid. Can't you see that?"

"Yeah, I can see. But it doesn't make it any easier. I'm running out of options."

Davina couldn't help but mother him. "How are you coping?"

"I'm sleeping in a park, with the mankiest tramp in town acting as my valet and going to the shops for me."

"Oh, you poor thing. Kill the painting, Hugh, it's not worth it."

"No way! No how! The Stormer lives."

His ferocity frightened her but not so much that she didn't admire him for his guts. "Okay okay. Listen, I'll help. Anything I can do. Till Crawford calms down. He can't keep up this lunacy forever." They reached her car and she unlocked doors. "Now," she asked, "what park are you residing in?"

In the Dog's Breath Midden and the bikers were quietly drinking and minding their own business when Fiona stormed in and planted herself in front of them.

"Where is he?" she demanded. "You said he was coming round to apologise. Humbly, and on his knees, and he was going to paint over that big tart."

Midden's career with the U.N. was vaporising. "Now, FiFi, I didn't say that."

"Well, it's the only way I'll take him back," she insisted.

Midden shrugged. "I'll let him know. When I see him."

But that wasn't enough for Fiona. "Where is he then? Shacked up in some smart hotel with his fancy woman now he's got money in his pocket?"

Midden couldn't let that pass, even from his sister. "You know that's not Hugh's style. Anyway, none of the hotels will take him, not since that cop barred him from everywhere."

"Serves him right."

Midden tried to revive his diplomatic career. "Maybe you should just leave him alone for a while, Feef."

This only served to spark her. "Do you know something I don't? Where is he?"

"I haven't a clue, he's lying low till the cop cools off."

This didn't fulfil her deep need to squeeze testicles "Somebody knows. You ..."

She pointed at Tank,one of the bikers, and stamped her foot. "..where is that wee bugger?"

The biker shook his head and backed off, so she turned on another. "I'll bet you know ..."

This one too backed off. Fiona screamed, "You're all in it together, you men. You're scum, filth ..."

She stamped her foot one last time, put her handbag on the table and sat down, opposite her brother. "And I don't suppose anybody's going to buy a lady a drink?"

As they drove to Hugh's park, Davina continued her interrogation. "There must be a bed and breakfast or something."

"Not even a homeless unit. When your man does a job, he doesn't mess about."

Davina was unconvinced. "I can't believe ..." She shook her head.

"My local, where I've been drinking for twelve years won't serve me. My local councillor denied I was on the voting roll." The car pulled up at red lights.

"Crawford's gone nuts," Davina said, "it's the only explanation."

"Well, you married him," Hugh accused.

Davina drew him a dirty look, but Hugh continued digging the hole. "Are you telling me you didn't know what he was like?"

"Not this bad," Davina said weakly, "Never this bad."

Hugh searched for more. "Is there something else going on, something that would make him react like this?"

"He's missed out on a couple of promotions, but ..." She looked up at the traffic signals.

"Come on lights."

"In a rush?" Hugh asked, "Do you really have to get his dinner ready?"

Davina sighed. "I'm a housewife. A homemaker. I accept my role."

"Yeah."

It was dangerous territory that Davina felt uncomfortable with. She steered the conversation away. "Maybe you could move away, just till he gets it out of his system. London or something."

"Hey, I admit I'm feart, but I'm no' that feart."

"No, seriously, somewhere he doesn't have any power."

Hugh shook his head. "He's got more power than you can imagine."

"What is wrong with these lights?" and her voice was rising to a whine.

Outside, the roads were clear, but the lights remained red.

"Let me show you how much power," Hugh said. "Watch this."

He got out of the car and closed the door behind him. The lights turned to green. He got back in again and they immediately reverted to red. He got out again and said, "Go home, I'll walk."

She wondered what he was up to but Hugh had noticed something she hadn't. He waved her away and finally, she took the hint and drove off.

Hugh waited till she was out of sight then turned and ran from the approaching police van.

8. THE RUN

He was up and running and his brain was null and void. For some reason he knew he had to make it to The Stormer. She would protect him, surely. In any case, he had to escape, but in that abnormal way he knew that the best way to escape was to stand there and take hanging and drawing and quartering. All the punishments they could give, there was that much masochist in him. But for all his spirited words, when the whip came upon him he ran like any other beast. He dodged people in Victoria Road, and behind him, distant still, a siren was beginning its vengeful whoop.

Songs came flying at him, and all the days and all the times, and every bleary moment it passed. It was as if he was drowning, that fast picture search of his life. In the world of mental deficiency, the dumpling is king.

"Hullo there, Mrs Smith. Got your youngest married yet?"

Whoo, whoo, pace yourself now, son, don't expend your energy too quickly. Who knows how far you'll have tae run - to the magical moon, my friend, and back, if the notion takes us. Don't do a daftie on me now, Hugh, brother mine, there's a battle to be fought and a maiden to be won.

That's what you wanted all your dull life, to live in

cinemascope, and now it's here you're shitting yourself.

Do heroes get time and a half for working Saturdays?

"Ho, Peter, your wife dropped the wean yet? Half price nappies? You've got to be kidding."

A roar from the telly through an open window. Was there football on the telly? He hated that. Who'd scored? Was it a roar of joy, or disbelief, the jammy bastards.

And now.

Hugh Cooper dodges and weaves past the defenders, running the race of his life, this man is poetry in motion, and yes, he's putting the pressure on now, and he's broken his opponent's spirit.

Whoosh goes Hugh Cooper, and me maw me maw me maw goes the Mad Skwad, and splang goes Mrs Hopkin's shopping bag.

"Sorry, Missus, aw help, gies a break, gaun tae stop beltin' me wi' yer brolly. Now listen, I'm a peacable man, I said I was sorry, whit you doing with a french loaf anyway, a woman o' your age, just you stick tae a square loaf, same as your mammy used to buy."

Whoosh.

Life is just a condemned cell. Love is just a drunken notion. Swap at will.

Women who shave their armpits are witches cutting down on wind resistance during flight. I'm Beelzebub - Fly Me.

Sorry, Great White Mother, bad taste. Ye see, ah do care. Christ, Vicky Road wasn't this long the last time ah didn't run up it.

If I get ye the wool will ye run me one up tae?

Bloody marathons, by fuck, I feel as if I'm running a lap of honour.

Stop swearing, Hugh, it shows a poor command of the English language. Aye, but maw, ah like swearing.

Skelp.

"Aye, it's me, Hugh Cooper."

"Don't try to be funny, Cooper, it doesn't become you." A teacher had once said that to him, stigmatised him for life. I hope you're dead, Cocoa Brown, that's how funny I can be, you smart bastard, and stick your physics up your arse.

God, if you love me, turn me into a helicopter *now!!!*
See.

Elvis. Hendrix. Lennon. Ah hope they're rocking in heaven.
See me. See ma man. See mince. He loves it. Oh Glasgow.

Highest percentage o' teetotallers in Britain, stick that in your
25 mls, the drunken Scots. The reason we drink so much is
'cause we've got a drink worth drinking.

The dear green place. Dear? Only the rates.

"Will you weans bugger off an' stop running after me. Here's
me running for ma life, an' youse think it's a game. Aye, I'm
the wan that paints the dirty pictures, and no, you're no' gettin'
an autygraph."

I wonder if the Mad Skwad would accept keys till I have a
pint? I mean, fair's fair, they're only human.

No, they're not. Whoosh.

Why didn't I emigrate to America when my Auntie Jean asked
me to?   Cos it's no' Glasgow. That's the trouble wi' most
places.

I wonder who's the roll models in a bakery.

I'll need to gie up the fags. Or cut down. Or switch to low-
tar.

I bet I've got the most sensitive nipples o' any man in Glasgow.
It's a fact, my nips are like a Cammy Souter aw tae themselves.
Where's this big fat wifie gaun?   Jeeze, they should build a
by-pass round her.   Bet she's goin' to the health club tae work-
oot wi' Jane Fondle. "Go for the burn, hen!"
Zoom.

Me maw me maw me maw me maw me maw me maw me
maw me maw me maw - here they come, bunch o' weans.
Right, watch this, jump over the fence at St. Andrew's Cross,
an' where does that leave youse? You'll need to go all the way
round.   And this is where you should dive up a close, Hugh,
and make yourself invisible to the world in Glasgow's
encompassing womb.

No chance! Go for glory.

Up Eglinton Street goes the small but immaculate figure of
Hugh Cooper, his head held high, his wee legs working like
pistons. Have you any sympathy for this man, the plight he's
in, this itinerant artist, this stand up idiot?

Watch your mouth, you.

Kiss yer ass, yer ass, whatever will be, will be.

No Mean City?   Ah, but they got it wrong, it should have been No Seen Mitty, cos that's all it is, a city of Walter Mittys, wee men wi' big ideas. No seen him? Couldnae miss him.

If I had a penny for every time I'd spent a penny I'd be a rich man.

"How's it goin', Jake? What am I doin'? I'm runnin' for ma life, the Mad Skwad are after me. Have a nice day?   Oh aye. Wunnerful."

I wish I had a sugary doughnut, my energy level's dropping way off.   Maw was right, always start the day wi' a good breakfast.   Come on, International Rescue, if you're going to show up, now's the time.   Mah wee pins is knackered.

Well, sod you an' Lady Penelope.

Cut left up Kilbirnie St, they're hot behind you.   Imagine getting a doing on the South Side.   Aye, ahm a sooth sider. Ye look mair like an ootsider.

There was a chance!

If he belted up West Street he could double back and make it to the Clyde through the back closes.   But they were so near behind him, and he was so tired.

Oh God, do me a favour now.   And the traffic closed round the Mad Skwad, a learner in a sweet little Citroen stalling.   It gave him seconds, no more.   He was there.   The game was a bogey

Whizz.   Deep breaths now, slow down, heart thumping.   It wasn't good for your health to take violent exercise after bevvying. He'd read that somewhere.   Probably written by some bum fluff sitting in an office who'd never been chased by the Mad Skwad.

But he'd forgotten radio. As he turned the corner to what he imagined was safety another van-load of the Mad Skwad were waiting for him.

Hugh didn't even consider running further. He walked straight to the van and climbed in, assisted by rough calloused hands.

He curled into a ball on the van floor and said, " No' the face, lads. I'm doing a self portrait next week."

The Mad Skwad kicked him in the head and he passed out.

The massage parlour was in a quiet cul-de-sac and, apart from a discreet sign, looked no different from the houses surrounding it. Men pulled up in cars and entered the premises and others left. Crawford, in civvies, approached furtively, but just as he got to the door some men were leaving and he marched straight past. He walked on a piece, turned about and walked back. At the door he paused, and the strain of what he was about to do blanched his face. He shoved open the door.

Before long a very nervous Crawford was sitting on the massage table. He was naked, apart from a towel draped over his lap. Fiona entered, dressed for work.

"What'll it be?" she asked.

Crawford didn't have a clue. "Oh ... everything," he said weakly.

Fiona nodded and flexed her fingers. "Okay, lie down. Face down."

Crawford complied and Fiona poured oil on his back and started massaging. After a while Crawford closed his eyes as he started enjoying it and had to pull himself together.

He tried to initiate some conversation. "This is my first time, you know. In one of these places."

"Oh aye, where do you normally go?"

"Nowhere! I don't go anywhere."

"So what is it, your birthday?"

"Yes ... yes, that's what it is, my birthday. I'm treating myself."

"Many happy returns."

She poured more oil on his back in honour of the occasion.

"I might treat myself a little bit .. more," Crawford ventured.

Fiona nodded. "Aye, you should get out for a drink or something. Bugger, the oil's done. I'll be back in a tick."

She walked out and Crawford jumped to his feet. He reached for his clothes, took out his police notebook and made a few quick marks. As he was putting the book back his handcuffs fell from his pocket. He held them for a moment, considering whether to keep them out, before thrusting them hastily back into his trousers. He was barely on the couch again before Fiona returned. She rolled him over and started massaging his chest.

"Do you do ... extras?" Crawford croaked.

77

Fiona made a face. "Roll and sausage, tea, coffee, soft drink, scrambled egg on toast ..."

"Is that a code?" Crawford asked.

"No," Fiona replied, "it's a joke."

"Well, I meant .."

"I know what you meant."

She continued pummelling at him, annoyed now.

"Well, do you?"

"You asked for me by name. The receptionist thought you knew me."

"No .. no .. just, someone recommended you."

"Obviously not a regular, or they would know."

"Know?"

"That I don't do ... extras."

"Oh."

She continued working on him, and then sighed. "Listen, I'm sorry. I'm just in a foul mood, that's all. Problems in my personal life. It is your birthday after all. What do you fancy?"

This threw Crawford who was not well versed in such matters. "Oh .. ehm .. eh .. what's the worst thing on offer? The dirtiest, vilest, filthiest act ..."

"Oh, right. Something you can tell your grandchildren about when you're old and grey?"

"I don't have ..."

"Aye, I know, of course you don't. You want something ... way over the top?"

"The most unnatural thing you've got." And his imagination strained with delight as he prepared to pounce on her for her debauchery.

"Are you sure?"

"Absolutely. As you said, it is my birthday."

She gave him a playful slap on the thigh. "Okey dokey."

She wiped her hands and headed for the door.

"Where are you going?" Crawford asked, suddenly worried.

She stopped with her hand on the door handle. "Like I said, I don't do extras, but some of the others do. Unnatural, you said?"

She opened the door and shouted out, "Arthur! Client for you!"

His mind swam. He was on the pillion of Midden's bike.

"Yer losing Glasgow!" Hugh's voice was panicked.

"We're going for the space warp, wee man. Don't worry, we'll be all right when we come out the other side."

It was roared to Hugh, but half of the words were still drowned. Glasgow was flashing by, the street lights a continuous line, the buildings blending into dark monoliths.

A green light flicked to amber, Midden twisted the throttle, the light jumped to red, the fat rear tyre bit into the wet road and blasted them across the intersection. A taxi's brakes squealed in complaint.

"You tryin' to kill me?"

Hugh tapped him on the shoulder and told him to stop somewhere. Midden came down the gears and cruised up towards Brigton Cross.

"Hasn't half changed, eh Hugh. We had some times here."

Hugh was silent, looking up at the flat where he'd grown up. His mother and father, both gone now, the dreams they'd held for him. He felt sick.

And what did those four walls hold now? Another family? Another lifetime? Another cauldron of hopes, fears, wishes and despair.

"Hugh?"

I'm sorry, maw, dad, I never did nothing while ye were alive. Wasted my time, maybe. Certainly didn't please you. Didn't mean to hurt you.

"Hugh?"

Changed now. Did something. People know my name. I'm somebody. Means nothing.

"Hugh, ready to go back now?"

Jeeze maw, I'm scared. Don't know why. Nothing's threatening me. Nothing immediate anyway. They've done their worst. And even if there's more I can handle it. Just ... what if I made a mistake, maw? I'm getting grey hairs, maw, I'm getting old. I can feel the fire fading. Not out yet, not by a long shot, but I can feel the flicker. There's nobody left, nobody to cry out my triumph too. Nobody to bury my head in. Get a trade. Get security. Get married. Get kids. Thought you were crackers, folks. But you knew, didn't ye. God, I'm so lonely.

"Hugh. Are you all right?"

It's like failure was my only friend, and now it's gone, I've got nothing. Half a life's apprenticeship for one painting. Aw the fuss they're making about it. A policeman's wife in the scud. Damn all about its quality. What does The Stormer say? It's the dream, maw, it's the Hugh Cooper statement.

"Hugh, I've been struck dumb by some beautiful sights before, but never Brigton Cross."

Noises brought him back. Noises he didn't know and which didn't compute with his expectations. There was a voice. It said, "Road traffic accident" and he wondered what that meant. Slowly pain seeped into him. His ribs, his back, his sides, his head, there didn't seem to be a part of him that was unplayed by that orchestra.

"Don't try to move."

Who said that?

He opened his eyes but there was only a white glare and it hurt. He closed them quickly.

Somebody was sticking something up his nose. Get the fuck away from my neb!

But the swab cleared out his nostrils and allowed him to smell and he knew where he was, a hospital.

"Whath happened?" he asked without moving his painful jaw.

Luckily the nurse was conversant with this language.

"You were hit by a truck, Mr Cooper."

Oh aye?

"A very big truck. You've got multiple broken bones, a concussion and god knows what else. But you'll be okay. Don't worry."

He shook his head as far as he could manage. "Sno truck."

"Yes, Mr Cooper, a truck. The policemen that brought you in said it was a truck."

"Lying bathtard."

Her boyfriend was a cop so she knew this to be true, but she chose to ignore it.

"Ish The Shtormer okay?"

"Who?"

"The Shtormer. Painting. Mural."

He heard whispers.

"Are you Hugh Cooper, the artist?"

"No, just a guy got hit by a truck."

"It is. It's him. I saw him on the telly," another voice said.

"We're big fans," the first voice whispered into his ear.

"Need to see. Eyes hurt when open them."

"That will pass. Just rest."

"Why?" he wheezed.

"Sorry?"

"Why like The Stormer?"

She seemed surprised. "It's a wonderful, beautiful painting, Mr Cooper. You should be very proud."

Again, he shook his head as far as he could manage. "No no, lots beautiful paintings. People *like*. People *love* Stormer. Need to know why."

"Well, we're no art critics."

"Xactly. Don't know art. Don't know me. Why love?"

There was a further whispering session and he felt himself drifting off, but he was desperate for an answer, he dug in.

"We don't know, Mr Cooper. Mr Cooper?"

He stretched his jaw and felt a click. The pain receded. "Gonnae call me Hugh, for fuck's sakes, I'm not a bank manager."

"Well, Hugh, we don't know why we like the picture, we just do. She's a beautiful woman. You must have loved her very much."

Hugh managed a weak smile through the wires holding his jaw together. "Loved her? Didn't even know what love meant, Never even kissed her."

Again there was whispering and he hated that, not just that he couldn't join in, but that he couldn't see them.

"We thought," the nurse said slowly, " that .. that .. it was a lost love. Somebody you'd cared for. That's what the papers implied."

"But to see her, was to love her," Hugh croaked, "Love but her, and love for ever, Had we never lov'd sae kindly, Had we never lov'd sae blindly, Never met-or never parted, We had ne'er been broken hearted."

"What was that?"

"Bit of Burns. Ae Fond Kiss."

"It's beautiful."

"Aye. He knew his stuff, our Rabbie."

"Rest now."

And he did.

Hugh was painting again and shade and tone and perspective fell into place as if he'd never had any doubts.

"Now, there aren't many artists who use raw linseed oil, Hugh, but it's always been a favourite of mine. I think its darkness gives it a certain quality. The flax is heated with steam, you see, before the raw oil is pressed out of it. You get more oil that way, and it's more durable."

Oh, shut the drivel and let me paint. I don't want to know about technique and the history of the development of materials. Programme all that shit into a machine and let it create art. All the art I'll ever have is in me, and you can't put any more in.

There were more flashes of coherence, conversation, lucidity, but he didn't know which were real and which imagined. Had Davina come to see him? Fiona? Midden? The Shame? No, they'd never have let him in, not with hygiene rules. But The Stormer had definitely come. He remembered that well.

"What have they done to you?"

"They have tried to crush me and failed. I defy them."

"As you must. You are the maker."

"I am small and ill-formed, Stormer. You are what must live."

"I? What am I that I must bear this burden?"

"You do not know your destiny?"

"I am nothing. I am paint on a wall."

"And that would make those that tend me love you?"

"That, I do not understand."

"Nor I, though it becomes clearer."

"Enlighten me, for I must know my purpose."

"No need, I have imbued you with my purpose."

"I must know to make me complete."

"You are hope, Stormer, nothing more, nothing less."

"Hope for what?"

"Hope for all. It was all I had to say and I said it."

"Brave, proud man, my maker."

"Broken man for now."

"They cannot break you. They shall not. The Stormer says ….." and he drifted away again.

Finally, a week later, he could open his eyes without a piercing headache, and was happy to see that his nurses were all pretty. Small celebrity that he was they were glad to look after him and pleased to talk. What they didn't like was Midden trying to feel them up when he came to visit.

"NHS. Free at the point of delivery," he explained.

"Leave the lassies alone, you lecherous bastard," Hugh complained.

"Oh, so you've got exclusive rights to the skirt? I'm entitled, I pay my taxes…."

"No you don't"

"Oh aye, right enough. Anyway, how ye doing, wee man?"

"Been better."

Midden shoved a bag into the cabinet beside Hugh's bed. "Brought you some grapes."

Then whispered. "Well pressed and fermented. Bottle of red. Screw tap, in case you didn't have a corkscrew to hand."

"Thanks, pal." Hugh struggled to sit up and a nurse came rushing over to help him with an extra pillow.

Midden pulled over a chair and straddled it. "They say it was a truck."

"Aye, a truck called the Mad Skwad."

"Bastards!"

"I knew it was coming."

"This bastard Gillespie'll have set it up."

"No doubt, he just about admitted it to me when I went to see him. At your suggestion may I add."

"Aye. Sorry about that. Seemed sensible at the time."

"I don't come to you for sense, Midden, I come to you for madness."

"Well, we'll need to sort your boy out, Hugh. Give me a list of your injuries and we'll try to match them exact."

"No," Hugh barked with as much energy as he could muster.

"We stick together, Hugh, you're a brother, we take care of each other."

"I'm not a member of your poxy gang."

"Maybe not by the rules, but you've done enough artwork for us to make you an honorary member."

"Doesn't matter, I don't want you giving Gillespie a kicking."

"Why not, he's due it?"

"Because you and your boys don't do subtle, Midden. Half of you will get spotted and caught. And then there'll be jail time for some and harassment from here till doomsday for the rest of you. It's not worth it."

"Aye, hadn't thought of that."

"See, don't do sense, Midden, it doesn't become you."

"The Feef wants to come and see you."

"What, to gloat?"

"She's calmed down. She's feeling sorry for you. Let her back in, wee man."

"Can't be done. I'll always have time for her, but I can't go back."

"Fair enough, I'll see if one of the other boys fancies a romance."

"That's what I love about you, Midden, you really look after your kin."

"Listen, pal, if she's not got a man in her life she makes mine hell. She thinks I run that garage as a stud farm for her."

"Well, that's boosted my ego."

"No, you were different, Hugh. She really liked you. Wouldn't surprise me if she didn't let you go that easy."

"Easy? Don't make me laugh. And I *mean*, don't make me laugh, my ribs are still killing me."

"When do they reckon you'll get out?"

"I'm not rushing them. I've got nowhere to go."

"I'll try and find you a crash pad." He hesitated as if shy of asking, but finally forced himself. "Listen, has your fancy piece, the cop's wife, been to see you?"

Hugh shrugged. "Don't know."

84

"Don't know? Jeeze, she's what's behind all this."

"I've been drugged up to the eyeballs for the past fortnight, Midden. You must know what that's like. I couldn't tell my arse from an artichoke."

Midden stood up and kicked the chair away. "Well, that's easy enough sorted." He waved over to the nurses' station. "Ho, miss, over here!"

When one of the nurses bustled over he growled, "Has The Stormer been here?"

The girl looked startled. "The Stormer? That's a painting."

"Aye, I know. The lassie it's based on, his floozy."

The nurse looked around her. "Her? Here?"

"Aye, hear hear. Has she been here to visit the man?"

She still couldn't come to terms with it. "Her?"

"Her name's Davina," Midden growled.

The nurse shook her head.

"She's only human, hen. Flesh and blood. It's just the wounded soldier here that's turned her into a myth."

"But here?" the nurse insisted.

"She's the reason Hugh's lying there half dead."

"Oh, was she driving the truck?"

"Fuck me, is everybody mad," Midden snarled.

And Davina Gillespie walked into the ward and twenty five jaws dropped simultaneously. She was wearing a tight green polo-neck jumper with black jeans and a long black coat streamed behind her. She strode with the confidence of the gorgeous straight up to Hugh's bed, swivelled neatly on one heel and perched her perfect behind on the edge of it. The nurse stared and stared and even the hard bitten Midden couldn't resist a perfunctory bow. Where entrances were concerned, the girl had it.

"Hi, Davey," Hugh said.

She seemed not to notice the effect her entrance had had. "I would have come earlier," she said, "I sent a card."

"Did you. I've been out of it."

"You stupid bugger," she suddenly snapped, "Why didn't you stay in the car with me? Imagine getting knocked down in the street."

"He didn't," Midden grunted.

She noticed his existence. "What?"

"Your man set the Mad Skwad on him."

"Who?"

"Special Operations Unit. Strathclyde Police."

"No, he wouldn't. He couldn't … be so petty." But her voice trailing away told that she didn't believe it.

The nurse dashed back to discuss the arrival of this new celebrity with her friends.

"Crawford said…" Davina began but Hugh shushed her. "It doesn't matter."

Her eyes filled. "Oh, Hugh."

Hugh pulled himself further erect. "C'mon, Davey, I'm still alive and it's not as sore as that time you clouted me round the ear at school."

"You shouldn't have stuck your hand down my blouse."

"I was looking for that toffee I'd dropped."

"I know what you were looking for," and she smiled. He passed her a tissue from the box he had at his bedside and she blew her nose. "I'm supposed to be cheering you up," she said.

"You are."

Midden cleared his throat, looking for acknowledgment.

"Sorry," Hugh said, "This is a friend of mine, Midden. Midden, this is Davina."

"Mid_den?" she rolled it about in her mouth

Midden scowled. "Had to have something to call myself seeing my folks didn't foresee the problem in calling a working class Glasgow boy Cecil."

Hugh heaved. "I told you not to make me laugh."

"I thought you knew," Midden protested.

Hugh shook his head wildly and clutched his ribs.

"But why Midden?" Davina asked.

Midden stroked his stubbled chin. "Because it suited me. It's the perfect name for a dirty biker, and that's what I am."

"Oh, I thought you were one of Hugh's artist friends."

"Hugh doesn't hang about with artists. He thinks they're wankers."

Davina seemed flustered. "But he.. he .."

"You don't know your man, do you, kid? Hugh might paint, but he's no' precious."

"No," she said quietly, "he's certainly not that. But you're right, I don't know him very well. Do I, Hugh?"

Hugh grinned. "It's Midden's most desperate wish that I should give up the last vestige of civilisation and join his motley crew."

Midden had the decency to look affronted. "Aye, but that's business."

Davina crossed her legs. "I don't understand."

"Midden here's a bit of a bolshevik, runs a communist system. Join up and you have to throw all your skills and talents into the pot. So I have to paint their petrol tanks and design their tattoos for nothing."

"Whereas, at the moment, he just robs us blind."

Hugh shrugged. "I admit it, Midden's boys have kept me alive over the years."

"And proud to do it, ya wee shite."

Davina recognised their comradeship and it gladdened her that this little man who had come crashing back into her life and set it alight had such good friends.

The nurse came over holding a postcard. "Would you mind signing this? And Mr Cooper as well, of course."

"I've signed dozens of them for you," Hugh grunted.

The nurse reddened. "Those weren't autographs, Mr Cooper. You wrote dirty things about nurses. But you were still doped up, so we forgave you."

Now Hugh reddened too. Davina took the postcard. "What is this?"

It was The Stormer.

"They're selling them down at the Barras," the nurse explained. "There are T-shirts too."

It was a strange feeling, becoming an icon, and Davina didn't really know how to deal with it."

"Getting one signed by both of you would be really special," the nurse pleaded.

"Oh aye," Midden agreed, "Worth a fortune to a collector."

The nurse was genuinely insulted. "I wouldn't sell it for the world!"

Davina accepted with dignity. She took a pen from her bag and signed Davina Gillespie across the back of the card. She handed it back to the nurse who looked disappointed. "Could you not put The Stormer?"

This made Davina uneasy. "I'm not The Stormer. That's a painting."

The nurse flashed a look at Hugh, as if he could help. Still feeling guilty about passing dirty comments to her and her chums he reached over and stroked Davina's arm. "Just do it for the lassie," he cooed.

"You're putting me in a terrible position," she replied coldly, "To sign that as The Stormer implies that I am accepting that I am this superwoman you've painted, when I'm not."

The nurse didn't get it. "But I'd be proud to be The Stormer."

"No, I'm not that bigheaded."

She caught a twinkle in Midden's eye. "Is that false modesty?" he asked.

She shifted uncomfortably on the edge of the bed. "Okay, okay. I admit the picture is me. But it's idealised. It's this fantasy Hugh had of me. But he's never seen me washing dishes, scrubbing a floor, squeezing a spot. I'm not The Stormer, I'm Davina Gillespie, housewife, who makes lentil bake on Wednesdays and still can't hem a skirt. I can't reverse round corners, I constantly moan about the weather and I couldn't bake a cake to save myself. So where's The Stormer in that?"

The nurse was deflated. "I'm sorry, I didn't mean to …"

Hugh waved her quiet. "Davina. Tell a fib," he ordered.

Her eyes sparked.

"I mean it. These girls have cared for me better than I ever deserved. Nobody will think badly of you, nobody will reckon you're bigheaded. You're playing a role. It's like Clint Eastwood signing Harry Callahan."

She hesitated still.

"It's Hollywood," he continued smoothly, "The Stormer is a movie and you, the actress Davina Gillespie, are playing the title role. Now a fan asks you for a signature and wants you to sign as the character. It's not too much to ask."

This she could log on to. She took the card and signed it with a flourish. And another step in her evolution fell into place.

9. PAP

His bones still ached every time he came within fifty yards of a policeman, but he'd survived. Hugh and Shame were sitting on a park bench finishing off a Chinese take-away. Shame carefully licked the foil containers before saying, "Hugh, my boy, I am fair hoaching with calories. For a capitalist hyena, you're not a bad chap."

"What do you mean, capitalist hyena?"

"Well, I'm a wage slave, and you're paying my wages, so you must be one of the exploiting classes."

"Don't give me it, you've never eaten so good in all your life."

"Exactly. You should be President of the CBI. You're a fine example of a caring employer."

"Thanks very much, Shame, it's nice to be appreciated." He took out a packet of cigarettes, passed one to Shame and they both lit up.

Shame took a long deep puff and said, "Now, was there any mention of a pension plan?"

The next morning a letter appeared in the *The Herald*. It read as follows:

Sir,

I note with interest that of late Glasgow City Council has had a policy of trying to prettify the city by painting gable end walls with artistic murals. I am no opponent of art but feel that the most recent of these murals, the so-called Stormer goes beyond the bounds of decency in portraying an unclothed young woman. Nudity may have its place within an art gallery, but when portrayed so openly in public, where it may be viewed by all and sundry, and I am thinking here of the young and innocent, it is an affront to commonly acceptable standards. I urge the Council to reconsider their support of this artwork and have it removed or replaced

I remain, yours faithfully,

Charles Gorman

Who was, of course, Crawford Gillespie, stymied by the fact that despite his best efforts in hiding The Stormer, having Hugh beaten up and Fiona's reputation tarnished, that bloody painting was still up on the wall. He followed it up the next day with one to the *Daily Record*:

Dear Sir,

There is a painting up on a gable end wall in Glasgow that I think is disgusting. It is of a naked woman with no clothes on. What are we teaching our kids about morals and not running about naked when the Council is wasting our money by sticking big filthy pictures up on walls. I don't pay my rates for them to be wasted on pornography. I will never vote Labour again.

Caroline Gillis

And the following day he managed one to the *Evening Times*:

Dear editor,

What does Glasgow City Council think they're playing at with that bloody Stormer thing? My grandmother lives round the corner and has to see that disgusting thing at least five times a day every times she goes out. She is in her eighties and is not used to seeing bums and boobs up on gable end walls. This is not Edinburgh and we don't need any arty farty bare bums up on walls to tell people we've got culture. I intend starting a campaign to have this painting removed and if anybody would care to join me in this I would appreciate it if they could get in touch with me via your paper, which is tops and the best evening paper in Glasgow.

Colin Garfield

And there he ran out of steam. He'd guessed that public opinion was the best weapon he had against The Stormer, but was loathe to admit that he was instigating any action against it since it had become common knowledge that She was his wife. To his chagrin the only response he got from his plea in the Times was a letter from an Archie Blackwell who agreed with him entirely about the unsuitability of The Stormer.

He wrote as follows:

Dear Colin,

I read your letter in the paper and you are spot-on. There is to much muck on the telly as well nowadays and though I am no prood the thought of a big naked womman up on a wall fills me with disgust. Is this what we fouhgt the war for? If I can help you with your campain please get in touch with me.

Archie Blackwell

Crawford saw immediately that he could use Archie, though illiterate, as a front man in his war. He was the perfect candidate, thick, and obviously a man of the people. With him in the vanguard Crawford could remain in the shadows. He phoned the chap immediately and arranged to meet him in Bellahouston Park.

Archie Blackwell was a small, wizened man of about sixty with a bald head, a stoop and bad skin but he liked Crawford immediately.

"We'll have that painting down within the week, my lad," he promised. "It takes strong men to stand up to the forces of decadence and you seem like the very chap to be carrying the flag."

"Ah, that's the thing, Archie. I'm in a very sensitive position, job-wise. And I can't be seen to be leading this campaign. I think you're the man for the job."

"Me? Och no, Colin, it need s a fit young man like yourself to be doing these kind of things, not a done old man like me."

"Not at all, you're in your prime. You've got the wisdom, the maturity, and people appreciate that."

"Are you sure?"

"Absolutely. But don't worry, I'll always be there behind you, to give you support. And finance, if its needed." Archie's eyes widened, while Crawford continued with, "Together we'll raise the masses and let their voice be heard."

Archie shivered nervously. "As long as you're sure. But you'd better know that I'm no expert at dealing with the media and all that stuff. I'm a baker actually, but that'll be helpful."

Crawford failed to see how baking skills could be brought to the table and voiced his doubts.

"Because I work early," Archie exclaimed, "I'll have the afternoons for PAP activities."

"PAP?"

"People Against Pornography," Archie exclaimed, "It's only me and the lady wife at the moment, but with you on our side, and a concrete enemy in the form of this Stormer picture, we'll soon have all of Glasgow's good people flocking to join."

"I can't join your little organisation I'm afraid. I must insist on remaining anonymous," Crawford said, "If you can accept that we can move forward."

Archie nodded almost absent mindedly then said, "Five pounds annually."

"I'm sorry?"

"Membership fee for PAP. Even as an anonymous you'll have to pay."

Crawford remembered the money the Slab episode had cost him and quite gladly handed over a blue note. "What will be our first move?" he asked.

"We need more members. More members mean more money and with money we can take action."

"Undoubtedly. But that five pounds will buy you a few stamps, so I'd suggest you begin a letter writing campaign going with the newspapers and the Council and perhaps we can start getting some action that way."

The old man nodded in agreement. "Letters. Yes, that would be a good start. Problem is, I'm not very good with words."

"I'd noticed. I shall write the letters, and you can sign them."

"Capital!"

Rita Writes:

To say that I am appalled by the recent letter-writing campaign against Hugh Cooper's The Stormer would be to understate the depth of my feeling. I sensed when the painting was unveiled that there might be some kind of moral backlash at this blatant display of nudity on a Calvinist Scottish street, but that it has taken so long to emerge strikes me as either an inability on the part of these self-appointed moral guardians to face up to those who love this wonderful piece of art, or as some more sinister plot to attack The Stormer for reasons of their own. Is there some hidden anti-Stormer agenda that I am unaware of? Why, months after its appearance has The Stormer provoked such fury now? She is certainly not any more naked today, as I checked only this morning, and she is as brilliantly beautiful as she always was.

So, what do these People Against Pornography have against this gorgeous creature? The definition of pornography is a creative activity of no artistic value with no other aim but to stimulate sexual desire, and that is certainly not true of my girl. Naked does not mean pornographic in my book and I'm sure most Scottish people would agree with me. These PAPs are therefore picking on the wrong target. Pick on someone your own size, people, because The Stormer is way too big for you to take on.

And so Crawford's attempt to get the great Glaswegian public on his side was launched. It was slow, after mere weeks they had a membership of eight, all members of Archie's family, but with each one sending ten letters a day to the newspapers, radio and TV stations and the Council, each written by Crawford, something had to give. Eventually the Council declared that they would hold a public consultation meeting in Partick Burgh Halls about The Stormer and invited Hugh along to defend his work.

Hugh knew he was no speaker and, at first, said that he would attend and answer questions, but would not make a speech. But Cllr Murphy, who was to chair the meeting, told Hugh that it was an opportunity to make a statement and that not to do so would leave his enemies in the ascendant. Hugh could see where he was coming from, but still doubted that he could stand up in a hall full of people and pontificate. Put them in a bar and him with a dozen vodkas down his neck and sure, but to face them with nothing but words was asking too much. He was a painter, not a words man, but he phoned Rita and she took pity on him and wrote him a speech. This is what he said:

"What is the function of art? What is it meant to achieve? Why do we bother creating it and why do people bother looking at it or listening to it?

Here's what I think. I think the artist's job is to move people, to affect their emotions. Whether that's a horror writer scaring you or a comedian making you laugh, they're artists doing the job they were put on this Earth to do. So, would an artist ever set out to offend you? Yes, he would, if that was his intention. Offending his audience is a valid goal for an artist. Because, maybe by offending them with something, he's making them think about something.

So, it comes to this, did I paint The Stormer to offend anybody? And the answer is no. If The Stormer does offend anybody that was not its purpose. So, in that sense, as an artist I've failed to do my job properly. Because I wanted The Stormer to be a thing of beauty and an inspiration, because to inspire is just as valid as to offend. And if the people of this fair city of mine, which I love with all my heart, decide that I am a bad artist and I have not inspired them but offended them I will personally take a brush and obliterate The Stormer. I will always strive to be the best artist, the best painter, I can be, but I am not perfect, I can get things wrong.

But I ask you to look at The Stormer with an open heart. Is she not beautiful? She's certainly not ugly and to me ugly is offensive. Does she arouse you? That wasn't her primary aim, but if she does there's no shame in that, because God in heaven made women beautiful. And if she's naked, so what? Let's get offended by starving children, let's feel for the diseased, let's get passionate about the lame. But let's not get upset by a thing of beauty that shouts hope to the world. Yes, hope. Men hope to have her. Women hope to be her.

I shouldn't have to say these words, because they mark me down as a poor magician. The spell I cast with The Stormer did not say it all and so I have to appear before you to explain what should have gone into that lady and be obvious.

I ask you all, don't look at postcards, don't look at pictures in the newspapers, but go and look at The Stormer and judge her as she actually is. I shall stand by your judgment.

These words were reported back to Crawford by Archie and Crawford thought he had victory in his hands. The fool had literally handed it to him. To say that he would cover up the painting if the public demanded it was more than he could ever have hoped for. Every decent man and woman in Glasgow would vote for destruction.

But according to the phone-in vote organised by *The Herald* there wasn't a single decent man or woman in Glasgow.

10. CONFESSION

In the Dog's Breath Midden shouted round his cohorts and made a statement, "Party on Saturday night round my place."
There were shouts of glee and gratitude but Mixer cast a shadow. "What's the occasion, Midden?"
"Occasion? Fuck occasion, it's a party."
"You've never thrown a party in your life."
"I'll throw you out that window in a minute. Talk about looking a gift horse in the mouth. Out of the kindness of my heart I hold a party for my pals, and they want to know why."
He half turned away from the troop gathered round his table in mock disgust and pretended to sink himself in his pint.
Tank slapped him on the shoulder and said, "Don't let them get at you, Midden, I'd love to go to your party. Thing is I'll be a bit short by Saturday. For booze like."
"Don't worry about it, the drink's on me."
This cheered them all up and several more pints appeared on Midden's table.
"He's up to something," Mixer whispered to Tank.
"Who cares. Free drink."
"You're pathetic." Mixer floated round the assembly voicing his doubts but met with little success. Midden watched him and considered whether to intervene with a clenched fist, but it seemed that discretion was the better part of valour on this occasion. Despite that, he pushed his luck.
He stood up on a chair and further announced that he would be providing free food. This led to more acclaim but he then went and spoilt the effect by saying that only married men could bring their partners. This led to confusion and discussion till Mixer solved the puzzle.
"He's trying to get a lumber for Fiona!" he shouted.
"No I'm not," Midden reacted instantly, cursing his decision to push it.
"Aye you are. She's bursting your chops because Wee Hugh's chucked her and now you're trying to lay her off on one of us."
Midden continued his denials, but now that the notion had been placed in their minds it smelled too much like the truth to be ignored.
"I'll no' be able to make it," Chuck said, "I'll be washing my hair." He was bald.

"I'm babysitting my granny."

"I'm defrosting a roast for the Sunday dinner."

"Choir practice."

Midden listened to them renege one by one till only Smiley, the newest member of their biker gang was left. He heard him, with gratitude, agree to attend.

Mixer came over to him as he stood at the bar later and told him that Smiley was gay.

Hugh phoned Rita at *The Herald* and confessed his sins. "Thanks for the speech, Rita, you saved my life. But you caught me out in that last article you wrote, there is a wee vendetta against The Stormer."

"Oh my God, what do you mean?"

"The Stormer is based on Davina Gillespie, or Davina McLean as I knew her when we were at school. She married Crawford Gillespie who's now a Superintendent with the cops. He's not happy about me sticking his wife up on a wall in the scud."

"Oh, so he's behind this PAP campaign?"

"That's the least of it. He's barred me from getting served in all premises requiring licensing in Glasgow. That's why I was sleeping in a park. He's had me beaten up by some cop goons and my guy that watches The Stormer tells me there have been attempts to vandalise it."

"My God!" It was beyond her understanding and she repeated herself, "My God! Poor Hugh, what can I do to help. Shall I expose him? It might be awkward but I'm sure the power of the press.."

"No, that's not why I phoned you."

"But, dear boy, to have you beaten up, a policeman. We'll have him kicked out, the brute. You mark my words.."

"No, Rita, listen to me. Crawford Gillespie is not a problem. I could snap my fingers and have him kicked up and down Sausage Roll Street. That wouldn't solve anything."

"*The Herald* will pay for a security company to guard The Stormer. It would be a public service."

"No, the painting's not a problem either. There are people looking out for her, and sometimes I think she's looking after herself better than I can manage."

She took time to digest this. "So what can I do for you, Hugh?"

"You're the only sensible person I know that's not too involved, Rita."

"Oh dear, this sounds ominous."

"The problem is Davina Gillespie."

"But you said she was quite happy with the mural."

"I think I'm falling in love with her again."

"Ahh." She paused. "Of course it could be said that you never ever fell *out* of love with her."

"Aye, that could be said. Don't get me wrong, I didn't dwell on her, but what seemed like a stroke of genius, to make her the subject of The Stormer, has brought her back into my life again."

"I'm not an agony aunt, Hugh."

"I appreciate that, and I'm no lovelorn teenager. But the question is what to do now. Pursue or retreat?"

"Well, you've already taken a beating for her."

"No! That was for the painting."

"This can't be sorted over a phone call, I need time to think. Where are you phoning from?"

"I'm standing on the bridge on the Kelvin Way and I was singing Old Man River."

"I'll send a car for you. Have you eaten?"

"I'm fine."

"Okay, we'll get drunk. Wait there."

Ten minutes later a car pulled up and took Hugh to Rita's flat in Hyndland.

"You're a vodka man, aren't you?"

"Born and bred."

"Make yourself comfortable. Smoke if you want."

The house was warm and Hugh wondered if this was due to her age, but she was an excellent hostess. The drinks were delivered with crisps and peanuts and an invitation to kick his shoes off.

I've been thinking about your problem," she said finally, stretching her small frame out on a two seater couch.

"I didn't know who else to ask. Everybody else I know is in too deep to some degree or another. That's the dangers of being a lonesome cowboy."

"No man is an island, Hugh. But it sounds like you don't want to be alone any more."

"That's what I don't know. I've been in dozens of relationships, all sorts of girlfriends over the years, but I've never really connected."

"And you think this … Davina… might be the one."

"It seems like destiny, and that worries me."

"Yes, it would me too," and she sipped at her gin. She closed her eyes and seemed to be drifting away, but snapped them open suddenly. "I'm no expert on matters of the heart, Hugh. I met my husband when we were in our twenties. We married and had three children and he died five years ago. So, I don't have an elaborate romantic past to base any judgments on. I didn't even give my kids any advice when they were thinking of getting married. Does your Davina have children?"

"No, no Glasweeyins."

"Good." She got up and poured them both another drink.

"Now, you made a statement that you'd taken the beating for the painting, not the girl."

"Correct."

"And that's bullshit."

"Really?" He tried to sound calm, like a gambler caught out with a sleeve full.

"You could alter the painting so it wouldn't look like the girl?"

"Simple. But then it wouldn't be The Stormer."

"So who are you in love with, The Stormer or Davina?"

"That's why I'm here."

"We could dance about like this all night, Hugh."

"I'm not trying to be awkward. I'm looking for clarity."

"Does the girl have any feelings for you?"

"That, I don't know."

"I'd think that would be crucial to your ambition."

"She came to see me at the hospital after the doing."

"Did you tell her who was responsible?"

"She was told I was run down by a truck. I put her straight."

"And the reaction?"

"Didn't want to believe it."

"Mmm."

He didn't know what that meant.

"Do you thing think this policeman's going to let you waltz off with his wife?" she asked.

"He can only beat me up so many times. And it's not Davina he wants to hold on to. It's him. Or his image of him." He took another slug of his vodka and lit a cigarette while Rita mused. Suddenly Hugh laughed and dragged Rita out of her reverie.

"Sorry," Hugh apologised, "Just thought about me sitting here with a *Herald* columnist. My mother would keep a *Herald* lying about the house for a week to let the neighbours know we were moving up in the world."

"I'm no fan of class differences but the broadsheets and the tabloids are growing closer by the day, and it's all downwards."

"Dumbing down? I still can't do the crossword."

"Don't worry, neither can I. But this isn't solving your problem."

"So what do you say, oh wise one?"

"You have to separate The Stormer from Davina."

"I can't."

"You'll have to," she insisted, "I predict nothing but disaster if you become involved with a dream. Dreams can become nightmares far too easily. The first time she lets you down your little world is going to collapse."

"I'm wise to frailty, Rita. The dream is what can be, not what definitely is. Surely half the fun is in finding out."

She drained her glass. "You seem to have it all worked out. I think you only came over to raid my vodka."

"Doesn't mean I'm not scared."

"Hugh, I haven't known you for long, but from what I've learned about you I'd think you're one of the bravest men I know."

"For taking a doing from the cops? Guys do that every weekend."

"I meant your struggle as an artist."

"I can't take credit for that, I don't know any better."

"Well, if you're driven, you just need to keep going. You don't need any words of wisdom from me."

"Maybe. Maybe I just need your blessing."

"Mine? Oh, Hugh, you'll make me cry."

He got up and poured them both another drink. "Let's drink to something."

"The Stormer?"

"She's had enough toasts."

"Okay, here's to Hugh Cooper and whatever it takes to make him happy."

"Weeks of work down the drain," Crawford complained to Archie.

"He's won round one, that's all. PAP doesn't give in so easily."

"The least you could have done is voted against him. Where was the massive support we expected? Not one single vote."

Archie looked embarrassed. "To tell you the truth, Colin, I was quite impressed with the painter fella. He wasn't half the degenerate I expected him to be."

"He is an utter degenerate," Crawford insisted, "He painted that monstrous picture."

Archie tugged at an earlobe. "Well, I took him at his word and went and actually looked at it. It's really quite tasteful. Have you seen it?"

"I've seen it," Crawford snarled.

They were sitting in Archie's living room and Mrs Archie brought through tea and biscuits and placed it on the coffee table between them. She perched herself on the couch beside her husband.

"A very pretty girl," she agreed with her husband, "and she's nude but she's not flaunting it, if you know what I mean."

"A good judge of porn, the lady wife," Archie said, slapping her on her scrawny thigh, "I think we picked the wrong target there. What say we attack the top shelf stuff in the newsagents?"

"No," Crawford barked.

"But Archie's done so much research," Mrs Archie whined, "He's got a stack of them upstairs."

"The Stormer," Crawford insisted, "That is our target."

"But, Colin, we live in a democracy and the people have spoken, they like The Stormer."

"Well, I don't."

"This is not a one-man band, Colin."

"It is when I'm the one paying for it."

"You seem a bit fixated on this Stormer," Mrs Archie said to Crawford passing him a jammy dodger.

Crawford recognised danger and had to waffle. "It's the public display that offends me. Top shelf stuff is exactly that, not easily accessible by the vulnerable. But that painting is beyond the pale, it can be seen by any passing man's wife or child."

"He has a point," Archie agreed.

"Do you have a wife yourself, Colin?" Mrs Archie asked and Crawford choked on his biscuit.

"No .. no," he spluttered, but Archie came to his aid, "We agreed that Colin would remain incognito," he reprimanded.

Crawford allowed Archie to thump his back to dislodge the crumbs from his throat and swallowed some tea for lubrication. "The thing is," he said recovering, "that we have to decide what we do next. Just because the majority are for that abomination doesn't make it right."

"You're absolutely correct. It's our duty to convince them of the error of their ways."

"But how?" Mrs Archie pleaded.

They sat and swapped stares till finally Archie said, "Knickers."

"Language, Archibald!" his wife said, flushing bright red.

"No, listen to me. We have this painter chap paint some knickers on the Stormer. Make her less vulgar."

"He won't do it," Crawford said sourly.

"Yes he will, yes he will," and Archie was bouncing up and down. "He seemed like a reasonable enough chap, didn't really want to offend anybody. I'll approach him on behalf of PAP and tell him, politely, that we *are* offended, and he could prove that he cares by adding some underwear to his painting. A bra and pants perhaps."

His wife was infected with his enthusiasm, "Yes, yes, it needn't be big, a g-stringy thingy."

"Which would allow him to fulfil his inspirational purpose and not offend us. It's ideal."

It didn't convince Crawford, she'd still be there, looking down at him. "Won't work. What's in it for him?"

"We'll pay him," Archie said decisively.

Crawford spluttered again, this time without the aid of a jammy dodger. "With what?" he demanded.

"Well, you're the money man."

Crawford remembered the amount of money he'd been prepared to spend on the paint fiasco, but that had promised obliteration and this only offered knickers.

"I'm prepared to put five hundred pounds towards bribing him," he said flatly.

Archie smiled. "Which only leaves us with the problem of tracking him down."

"He drinks in a pub called the Dog's Breath," Crawford informed him.

11. BRIBERY

Hugh and Midden were propping the bar in the afternoon when the old man approached them. He recognised Hugh from the meeting and sidled towards him, half pint shandy in hand.

"Sorry, pal," Midden was saying, "Still no joy in finding you somewhere to crash."

Archie moved in with his hand outstretched. "Mr Cooper. Wonder if I could have a word?"

Midden eyed him up and down and didn't perceive him as a threat. He moved back to make room for him. Hugh took the old man's limp hand and shook it.

"My name's Archie Blackwell and I'm the President of PAP."

"Good for you," Hugh said warmly, well used to the nutter-in-the-pub.

"People Against Pornography," Archie explained and Hugh groaned.

"I heard your speech at the consultation meeting and I was very impressed."

"You should thank the woman that wrote it, she might be in later."

"Oh, so it wasn't from the heart?"

"Every word of it, she got it spot on."

"Good, good. Can I buy you a drink?"

102

"Thanks. Large vodka."

Archie waved Bob over and continued, "The main thrust of your speech seemed to imply that you didn't intend to offend anybody."

"There's easier ways of pissing people off than painting a gable end wall."

"Of course, of course, but you must accept that you *have* offended some people or we would never have began our campaign against you."

"It would help that you're crazy. I think the vote proved that."

"There's no need to be insulting. We may be, as you say, crazy, but we are human and we do have opinions."

"Congratulations."

"I just wondered, Mr Cooper, if there was any possibility of a compromise between our two points of view."

"Like what, a lobotomy?"

"Come, Mr Cooper, there's no need for this. I know a decent man when I see one. I accept that your Stormer is a symbol of hope, will you accept that I find her nudity offensive?"

"Whatever turns you on."

Archie took a sip from his shandy. "The thing is, if she were a little less nude, she wouldn't offend me, and she would still represent your ideals."

"Says you."

"Would you consider painting over some of her offending parts? Some underwear perhaps?"

"No," Hugh said.

"A *very* small pair of briefs."

"No."

"Can you tell me why?"

"Because I agreed to paint a moustache and a pair of glasses on the Mona Lisa once and that didn't go down well. You don't get it, do you, Archie? The fact that she's naked is important. Naked means open. Nothing hidden."

"We are prepared to pay you."

"How much?"

"Two hundred pounds."

"That wouldn't even pay for the scaffolding."

"We'll take care of that."

Hugh shouted Midden over. "Guy here wants to pay me two hundred quid to put a bra on The Stormer."

"Tell him to fuck off."

Hugh grinned. "The people have spoken."

"We might manage a little more. Three hundred perhaps."

"It's not about money, ya old fucker," Midden growled.

Archie sniffed. "So, for all your claims to humanity you have no respect for those who don't agree with you."

"The greatest respect. If you don't like The Stormer, don't look at it."

"And that's your final word?"

"I'll no' be painting any underwear on her, and no ball gowns either. Tell you what, you respect my principles and I'll respect yours and we'll part as friends."

He held his hand out and, reluctantly, the old man took it.

"You're not a bad sort, I suppose," he said.

But Hugh was feeling magnanimous. "Where do you stay, Mr Blackwell?"

"Polmadie."

"I think you should live a little. Midden, give the nice old gentleman a run home."

And another one of Crawford's schemes crumbled.

Later Hugh was sitting in a bus shelter, but just for a change of scenery, because despite the beating nothing had changed, he knew no bus would take him. Davina's car pulled up and parked beside him. She got out, pulled bags from the boot and carried them into the shelter for Hugh.

"I can't stay long," she said, "Crawford's gone out. God knows where, he never goes out at night. I'm sorry I'm so late, you must be starving."

"Uh, I've eaten already. Shame got a burger."

She looked crestfallen. "I made it myself ... there's soup .. and pasta and ..."

Hugh took the bags. "Your own sweet hands, dear lady, how can I refuse."

She sat down beside him. "You shouldn't live on junk food."

"Why not?"

"It's not good for you. For your health."

"Why should that bother you?"

She knew what he was aiming for and gave him a little satisfaction. "Don't get clever with me, shorty, you know I care."

He cast his line again. "Do I?"

She stood up. "I have to be going."

Hugh pulled her back. "No. Stay. I'm sorry."

She allowed herself to be pulled back to the seat. "I'm sorry about what Crawford's doing to you, and I'm trying to help. What else do you want from me?"

Hugh looked at her intently and went dead-pan. "Proper crockery and cutlery. I've been eating out of tin-foil containers with plastic forks for so long I've lost the will to live."

She went equally dead-pan. "They're in the bag with the linen napkins and the bone china napkin rings."

"Thank God."

"Huh, I thought you were the wild man of art. A bohemian free-thinker who ate raw meat and drank wine from a goatskin."

"No, that's the other Hugh Cooper, the average artist. I'm often confused with him. Me, I'm a regular kind of genius. Can I tell you a secret?"

"Sure."

"I even kind of like country and western music," he said shyly.

Davina pushed him away. "You're sicker than I thought."

"Now, Watt," Crawford said, shuffling files, "we must find another way to attack our Mr Hugh Cooper."

Sergeant Watt was concerned about his own workload. "Sir, there are other matters we should be …"

"And lots of other police officers to deal with them. Our priority is the social terrorist, Hugh Cooper."

Watt recognised obsession but chanced his arm a little further. "I thought the ..err..Special Operations Unit had dealt with him, sir."

Crawford grinned coldly. "Special Operations Unit? Are they involved? News to me. I don't recall any request forms passing through my hands." He began flicking through Hugh's file again. "As I said, we need a new angle. Now, Cooper has these motorcyclist friends."

"Oh, tough bunch, sir, those bikers. And loyal, very loyal. Unlikely to get any joy from them."

"Yes, yes, I know all that. But they do have one weakness."

"Motorbikes, sir?"

Crawford shook his head, the master of hidden knowledge.

"Women?"

Crawford added a wide smile to his shaking.

"Drink? Drugs?"

Crawford paused for effect. "Easter eggs."

"Easter eggs?"

"These biking chappies try to curry favour with the general public by collecting chocolate Easter eggs every year and donating them to Yorkhill children's hospital."

"And you see that as a weakness, sir?"

Crawford thumped his desk with a balled fist. "Of course it is, man! You need money to buy Easter eggs. And money is one thing these drug-taking, fornicating, motor bicycling, layabouts don't have."

Watt leaned against the desk, suspicious of where this was going. "Money?" he managed weakly.

Crawford ignored him. "Yes, I think we can lure them into larceny, but as I'm known to Cooper I think it's your turn to play the agent provocateur this time."

Watt loved his desk, now his worst nightmare was coming true.

"It'll do you good to get operational for a while, Watt."

Watt steeled himself." "What do you want me to do, sir?"

"There's a pub where these chaps do their drinking, the Dog's Breath Bar."

Watt could see and smell it already.

"I want you to trot down there, in civvies of course, and lure these ruffians into our net by offering them what they so desperately want."

"What's that?"

"You tell them you've got a consignment you can let them steal and when they're about it we'll pounce and throw them all in jail, thus ridding society of a formidable menace."

"A consignment of what, sir?"

"Easter eggs, man! Are you deaf or stupid? You are an employee of an Easter egg manufacturer and have access to where they are stored"

Watt couldn't believe his ears, but thought quickly. "Where are we going to find Easter eggs?"

"I'm sure you can rustle up a few to tempt them into criminality."

"But there'd be no guarantee we'd get Cooper in our net, and he's our prime target."

"I know my man, Watt. He thinks he has a generous heart, and the thought of helping sick children will drive him to take part in this escapade. He won't be able to resist it."

Watt was caught between the devil and the deep blue sea. He needed to ask Crawford for an extra week's leave to take Mary on a second honeymoon, she'd been acting so strangely lately. It was an assignment he couldn't refuse.

He saluted and said, "I'm your man, sir."

The Dog's Breath Bar was just as ugly as Watt had imagined it. Garish photographs of semi-naked women adorned the walls and loud fifties rock'n'roll music blasted from an antiquated Wurlitzer.

He'd dressed for the part, but strictly on the level of his own imagination and limited wardrobe. He was wearing an open-necked blue shirt, an anorak, and Wrangler jeans with a knife-edge crease.

"Cop," Midden whispered to fellow biker, Tank.

It was the shiny black boots which gave Watt away.

He strolled to the bar with what he imagined was a confident swagger and ordered a beer. Leaning against the cracked formica counter in a casual manner he then sipped at it and grinned inanely round the crowded pub.

"What do you think he wants?" Tank whispered back.

"Maybe he's just in for a beer."

Tank shook his head. "Acting too suspicious. He's after something ..or somebody."

"Could be, but none of the boys are wanted for anything these days and you know we never bring recreational drugs into licensed premises."

Tank nodded. "You rule with a rod of iron, Midden. And just as well or half our guys would be jailed up."

"You're like the children I never had," Midden said.

He chanced a glance towards Watt again. "That's eighteen sips he's had from that pint and it's not down half an inch. Have a wander over and see what he's up to."

"Me? I don't know what to say to him."

"Just engage him in conversation, like any punter would. Talk about the weather or something."

Tank wasn't convinced but ambled over to the end of the bar where Watt was standing.

"Hello there, cold out, winter's drawing on, might be snow coming," he uttered.

Watt blanched.

Midden cringed.

Watt nodded slowly, staring into Tank's barrel chest. "Yes, but we had a lovely summer. And we're due a bad winter."

"Does it no' get awful warm for you when you're out on the beat?"

Midden closed his eyes in silent despair but Watt was on his toes. "I'm not on the beat anymore."

"Ah, so you *are* a policeman?"

Watt smiled. "Was, but well spotted."

Tank slammed his tumbler against Watt's. "We don't get many of the filth in here. Apart from the licensing police."

"I'm not a policeman any more" Watt lied convincingly.

"Bit young to have retired," Tank commented

"I was fired, I went rogue."

Tank was genuinely puzzled. "What's that then?"

Watt fashioned what he thought was a hard face. "A rogue cop is a cop gone bad."

Tank laughed, his slim frame shaking. "Youse are all bad. You're all bastards and wankers and chancers and .."

Midden, who had been listening, jumped up and squeezed himself in beside Watt before Tank decided to demonstrate how bad he thought cops were.

"Hello there," he smoothly, sticking out a hand, "my name's Midden, nice to meet you."

Watt instinctively shook his hand. "Sgt Watt. Ex Sgt Watt."

"Aye. Rogue cop. I heard."

He took Watt's arm and led him over to a table, waving behind his back for Tank to stay put.

"Forgive me for being pushy," Midden said, easing into a seat beside the policeman, "But this isn't a particularly safe place for a policeman, rogue or otherwise. So you must be wanting something."

"You're very astute, Midden."

"I've got medals for it."

"I'm a security guard now. The fact is I have some goods in the depot which might just be right up your street."

"Motorbikes?"

Watt couldn't face going through that game again so he jumped straight to the point. "Easter eggs."

This gave Midden pause. "Is that a new kind o' drug? 'Cause I've never heard any of the boys talking about shooting Easter eggs."

"No, genuine chocolate Easter eggs. All household brand names. Wrapped in silver paper and boxed. Understand you give them to the kids at Easter."

Realisation dawned on Midden. "Oh aye, *chocolate* Easter eggs. And you think we'd like to buy them?"

"I have the keys to the depot. You could just take them."

Midden shook his head. "They'd be off by Easter. Couldn't give the weans bogging old Easter eggs."

Watt hadn't considered this, but he took his time, sipping on his pint to give himself time to work round the problem. "They're in cold storage."

"Aye, in your depot. Where am I going to keep them?"

"I'm sure you and your friends all have fridges."

Midden leaned forward. "It's not half a dozen eggs we're talking about here. How many have you got?"

Watt, now in deeper than he wanted to be, grabbed a number from the air, trying to frighten Midden off. "Five thousand."

"Fair. What's the price?"

"They retail at £4.99, it's marked on the boxes"

"Fuck sake, I'm not planning on selling them."

Watt flinched at the expletive and said quickly, "I can lose the keys for a couple of grand. You'll have a window of about twenty four hours between me reporting the keys as lost and the company having the locks changed."

"Two grand? Okay." Midden reached into his pocket, pulled out a roll of £100 notes and peeled off twenty, which he placed on the table. Watt's eyes bulged.

"Sold a bike this morning," Midden explained. "Where are the keys? And where's the depot?"

Watt eyed the money hungrily but pushed his chair back and stood up. "Don't have them with me. But I'm fair. A grand when I hand over the keys and the rest once you've got the eggs."

Midden nodded. "You realise that if this is a stitch up I'll have to rip your arms off?"

"A stitch up?"

"Entrapment. A sting. A police set up."

"Why would you suspect that?" and Watt shivered nervously.

"Because in all my criminal career no-one has ever offered to let me rip off Easter eggs. They may be chocolate but they smell fishy, pal."

The sight of the two thousand pounds still seared on Watt's eyeballs. What a second honeymoon he and Mary could have with that kind of money. A cruise maybe. Or the Far East. The Bahamas. Or they could spend it on the house. They certainly needed new furniture, the kids had wrecked everything. He decided to brass it.

"Life is full of risks, Mr Midden."

"Oh, I'm aware of that." He pulled a small tape recorder from the breast pocket of his denim jacket. "That's why I've taped every word you've said. If this goes belly up, it'll stand up in court."

Watt nodded and left the pub on wobbly legs. He was approaching retirement and he wasn't going to risk his pension for Crawford Gillespie's vendetta. He'd tell the Superintendent that the bikers had refused his offer. And he would never go near the Dog's Breath ever again.

12. DOWNFALL

The following day a group of youths were loitering at the corner of the council housing scheme. CID officers Gibson and Robb pulled up in a battered old car a bit across the street from them. Gibson, in the driver's seat, checked his watch, just as a Porsche pulled up beside the youths. The youths moved towards it and Gibson and Robb watched a deal being done through the sports car's window. Gibson nodded to Robb and they reached for the door handles as a police squad car pulled up and parked in front of them.

The youths scattered in all directions and the sports car took off with squealing wheels. Gibson desperately tried to pull out after it, but the squad car blocked him. He jumped from the car with Robb at his heels.

Crawford, unruffled, climbed out of the squad car and walked towards them. "Now, lads, this time there's a chap I definitely want you to arrest. His name's Arthur and you won't believe ..."

Robb darted past Gibson, grabbed Crawford by the lapels and threw him over the bonnet of the car and pinned him there. "You fuckwit!" he screamed, "You utter, stupid, fuckwit!"

Crawford struggled to breathe and Gibson pulled Robb away. Crawford sat up, now thoroughly ruffled, and tried to sort his tie and uniform. "Y .. y .. you .. I'm a .. a .. superior officer," he stammered.

"In your dreams, you wanker," Gibson replied.

"You .. you ..can't call me that."

Robb sniggered. "Why not, everybody else does."

Crawford puffed up his chest. "You're on a report for this."

"Shut it," Gibson growled, "We're reporting you. For blowing our bust."

Crawford looked around him. "What?"

Robb enlightened him. "Aye, or did you think we were just sightseeing round here."

Crawford cringed. "It's just .. just .. just a genuine .. mistake .. nobody told me."

"They never told you because they don't like talking to you."

"You're a pest, Crawford, a pain in the arse," Gibson informed him. "A clown that gets on everybody's tits. Does that mean anything to you?"

"There's no need to be insulting."

"Oh aye there is. A great deal of need. We've had enough of your bullshit."

Gibson poked Crawford in the chest. "And your wee vendetta against the painter fella. Yeah, everybody knows about it. That's over. Get it? Over."

Robb followed through by sticking his face into Crawford's. "A real man would have taken that as a compliment on his pulling power. Fella paints his missus up on a wall."

"Just back off and leave him alone," Gibson instructed the Superintendent.

They turned away and headed back to their car. At the door Robb turned back to Crawford. "I hope wee Hugh is shagging her, you po-faced dick-head."

13. PHILANDERING

Meanwhile, at the home of our girl, Fiona's Volvo pulled up outside the Gillespie house and she marched directly up to the door and started banging on it.

"Come out here, ya dirty cow, and tell me where he is!" Fiona demanded.

The door was finally opened by Davina and the two women stood staring at each other.

"Can I help you?" Davina asked.

Fiona nodded slowly. "Aye, it is you, he got you to a tee. He might be a wee shite, but he can paint."

"I assume you're looking for Hugh."

"Oh 'Hugh' is it?" Fiona mocked. "Well, actually, it is. Hugh Cooper, my boyfriend, my fiancee."

"He never mentioned that he was engaged."

"Well he wouldn't, would he, no' when he's got a notion for philandering, no' when he's trying to fling it up you."

Davina looked down the street and saw net curtains twitching. "Would you care to come inside and discuss this?"

Fiona answered plainly. "Fucking right."

Davina led Fiona into the lounge and sat down on an armchair. Fiona refused a seat and remained standing, hands on hips. "On second thoughts," she barked, "there's nothing to discuss. He's mine and that's all there is to it. Now where is he?"

"I haven't the faintest idea."

"Crap. I know he's been sniffing round you."

Davina took a deep breath. "I'm sorry, I don't know your name."

"Fiona. Fiona Ferguson. And I'm not a tart," she replied hesitantly.

Davina raise an eyebrow but held out her hand. "I'm Davina Gillespie."

"Oh, not 'The Stormer'," Fiona mocked.

Davina ignored her. "I admit I have seen Hugh a few times since this all blew up. I've been trying to help him out. Especially as it's my husband who's caused all the bother."

"Helping him out by lying on your back?"

"Hugh and I are not having a sexual relationship," Davina said calmly.

"Oh, so you're not doing it? When Hugh and me first got together we were at it like the clappers. I couldn't walk for a week."

Davina didn't rise to the bait. "I'm sure that must have been very painful for you."

"Don't get sweety pie with me," Fiona snarled back. "If he's not shagging you, it's because he doesn't fancy you."

"I'm fairly sure he doesn't. Hugh's an intelligent man, I'm certain he realises there's no future in pursuing childish infatuations."

"You don't sound like you ever went to school with Hugh Cooper."

"Well I did," Davina answered. "I come from exactly the same background as Hugh. And you too probably. But I grew up, I evolved. Only don't ever make the mistake of imagining that I've forgotten my roots, or where I've come from."

She stood up, those long legs unwinding like pythons and her voice went guttural as she towered, this Amazon, over the smaller woman.

"And if you ever come round here again, shooting your mouth off like the arse end of an elephant and making bullshit accusations, I'll fucking snap you in two. Now get out."

Crawford's boss, Burroughs, was behind his desk facing his hapless underling who stood with his cap under his arm.

"Your behaviour's been strange, you can't deny that," Burroughs said. "Coning off streets, brawling in your office. There have been noises about victimisation. Serious, serious charges. And now this interference in a CID operation."

"I've been under a lot of stress, sir," Crawford tried to explain.

"Personal stress, Gillespie, personal. Nothing to do with the job. We all know about it, we're not unaware. But I wouldn't have gone to pieces if this painter chappie had put my wife up on a wall."

Burroughs turned the photograph of his horsefaced wife, which had been sitting on his desk, face down.

"He painted her naked, sir. That's what I found offensive."

Burroughs grunted. "But these artists don't think about naked women like we do, man. They're more interested in getting the light on their bottoms right."

"I'm only human, sir. I admit I reacted in a jealous manner, but I thought I was justified." Crawford pulled back his shoulders indignantly.

"Maybe so. But why you didn't just go over one night with a pot of whitewash and paint it over, god only knows."

Crawford tried to forget Slab and pretend he was appalled. "But that would have been defacing public property, sir."

Burroughs gave a resigned shrug. "Well, there's no way out of it, at the very least I have to enter a written reprimand into your disciplinary record."

"I was hoping you could avoid that, sir. There were a couple of senior posts I was thinking of applying for, and if my record shows ...."

Burroughs cut him short. "You're not going anywhere upwards, Gillespie. Cast that out of your mind right away. You're lucky I'm not suspending you, so your career stalls right here. Put in your years and take the pension."

Crawford's world collapsed. His legs buckled a little, but he held himself together. All the dreams he'd once had, all his ambitions, destroyed by a painting, destroyed by one man, Hugh Cooper.

"Yes, sir," he croaked.

"You're not a bad man, Crawford," Burroughs reassured, "but you've got to learn to relax. Now, we live in hope that this will all blow over soon with no damaging repercussions, but I want you out of the way for a while."

"Yes, sir."

"Get away for a week. Golfing. Clear out the tubes, do you a power of good."

Always one to seize the moment a humbled Crawford drove home immediately and began the process of packing suitcases, and hauling dusty golf clubs from under stair cupboards. Davina followed weakly in his wake. "Golf ? You don't even like golf."

"Chief ordered it. All because of that obscene painting."

"Don't start. We agreed not to talk about it any more."

"Davina!" and he seemed genuinely angry, "That painting is liable to ruin my life. What chance is there of me becoming Chief Constable now? If I keep my nose clean, do exactly what the Chief orders me to do, I might just be allowed to direct traffic."

"Is that all that matters to you, your career prospects?" but as she asked, she knew the answer already.

Crawford, of course, ignored it. "Come with me, Davina. It'll be like a second honeymoon. You needn't play, you can stay in the hotel."

"Yeah, you played golf the last time too. No thanks, I'm not the blushing bride any more, so if I'm going to be a golf widow it'll be in the comfort of my own home, thank you very much."

Crawford paused, then shrugged. "Whatever."

Half an hour later Davina watched Crawford throw his clubs into the boot of his car, climb in and drive off. She breathed a sigh of relief, she was free, at least for a while. Classical music had been playing softly in the background, but now Davina went to the sound system and switched it from Classic FM to CD. From behind some books on a bookshelf she extracted a Queen CD she'd hidden. She put it on and We Will Rock Ya blared out. She danced out, unbuttoning her rather staid blouse.

Dressed better and with no husband to tend to she dragged Audrey from her marital home and took her to see The Stormer. She'd never seen it in an evening light.

"Made any lifetime decisions?" Audrey asked.

Davina shook her head.

Audrey grinned. "A policeman's wife or an artist's muse. It's a hard call."

"What would you do?"

"Me? I'm not The Stormer."

Davina nodded sadly. "And I don't know if I want to be."

Audrey took her arm and they began walking. "You don't have any choice, Davina. From here till your dying day you're going to be The Stormer."

"He's cursed me with that, the little bastard," Davina spat out. "I wonder if he knew .."

"What he was doing?" Audrey, though younger than Davina, was more knowing. "Probably not. He's probably as trapped as you are. You were just two trains destined to collide."

"So you think I should go to him?"

Audrey stopped. "Do you want to?"

"I don't know!" Her voice was weak and pleading.

Audrey stepped away from Davina. "Go with the flow, kiddo. That way, if it goes wrong, you can blame fate and let it take the rap."

"You're a great help," Davina said, only half mockingly.

Audrey took Davina's hand and patted it. "So why ask me? I'm only a sexually-obsessed housewife with a husband and three kids. Ask her ..." She walked to her car, climbed in and drove off.

Davina was shocked at this sudden desertion, so unlike Audrey, who never did anything without calculated purpose. She turned her eyes upwards.

She went straight to herself. To The Stormer. She towered. She boomed. She dominated the city.

"Hullo, Stormer," Davina said.

"Hullo, Davina," The Stormer replied.

"How are you?"

"The same as always. The Stormer never changes. Never suffers the ups and downs of mortal clowning."

"No hate then? No love?"

"They would destroy me. Do you pity me for that."

"I envy you."

"Never that. Life's too short to want the clay so quickly."

"Are you mentor to me?"

"I am The Stormer."

"Yes, *you* are. I'm not."

"Be ambitious."

"I don't know how!"

"Remember your dreams, Davina. Remember the little girl, her wishes and wants, the ambitions she had .."

"A nurse? An airline stewardess?"

"Not careers, ambitions. Ambition is in striving, not achieving. Think lofty ideals, heroic adventure, fighting the good fight ..."

Davina's head ached. "I never had any."

"You buried them. You surrendered at the first battle and sought refuge in a safe castle."

"That's what they told me to do. I was an obedient child."

"It was not your destiny. Now you pay the price."

"It's too sore. Don't hurt me."

"Would I cause you pain, Davina?"

"By your very existence you do."

"But I only exist because of you."

"No, if not me it would have been another. Some blonde, some brunette, some saucy, swivel-hipped siren more worthy to bear the crown."

"You do yourself no justice."

"I am NOT you."

"I know. I only ask you to be YOU."

"But who am I?"

"The question that all ask. The maker has given you a guide, not a command."

But the moment passed and Davina was alone. Unsure, unfocussed, unused to the demands this new world made of her, she made amends, dipped her toes in purgatory, and prayed. She started walking.

It was a long time since Davina had seen the real Glasgow. She walked up to London Road from The Stormer and, just as some warped strand of karma had drawn her towards the mural, so now some longing for the excitement of the past called her towards Brigton.

The buildings of the Calton weren't covered in grime as of old.

They were gone. But evening was drawing on and it had begun to drizzle, some of it was just like old times.

There were still people in the streets. Old, shabby, people, with gap-toothed grins. And drunks, old and young, loud shouting, defending one's honour with saggy-arsed jogging bottoms that were strangers to dry cleaning.

The pubs, dark and dingy, promised their own magic. Open doors released a fog of stale beer. The varnish on the doors was black and cracked, and the frosted windows promised SALOON BAR.

Neon signs were coming on over chip shops, people gathering at street corners. Middle aged women in mini skirts and tank tops, fat flesh white and reeking of sweat.

If this is what I came from, why am I going back?

Because there's a re-charging of the batteries in returning to your roots. And your batteries need re-charged like nothing else. You need to remember who you are.

She didn't hurry, drinking in the rich soup of her past. Street corners showed names that haunted her - Green Street, Tobago Street, Abercromby Street.

Oh Glasgow, you terrified me then, hurrying home from the Guides, frozen, in the dark, thought everybody was looking at me.

And home, in the tenement flat, the room and kitchen you were safe again. Looking down, from three up, on the traffic blazing its lights down London Road. It was before the motorway, and everything from down south came along London Road. Articulated lorries, coaches, cars. What fabulous lands had they come from? Carlisle?

She laughed at herself, the naive child she'd been, and people did look at her. Wasn't she afraid now?

No, because now she admitted her love for that derelict heaven. You can't touch me because I love you. You can't assault me, rob me, rape me, kill me, because I walked through that valley of the shadow of death and, looking back, I had a fairly good time.

She went into the bar of a pub and perched herself on one of the torn vinyl stools. The barman sleazed over and said, "Hullo there, doll, what'll it be?"

She took her time, gazing along the gantry, "Shut yer face and give me a hauf."

She let the whisky last as long as she could then summoned the bar-man with a sweep of her lashes. "Do you know who I am?"

The barman eyed her nervously. "Eh ... no."

"Keep it that way."

"Aye ... right."

She slid off the stool and walked out, laughing to herself.

Darker now, lamp-posts were splashing orange, reflecting on the damp ground. The air getting chilly, a teenage girl throwing up in a close, another getting it thrown up her in another close, some things never changed.

But from Brigton Cross they changed dramatically. The renovators had been out and stolen her past. She could feel happy for these people, her people, who'd had the quality of their lives improved, but for her, inside she was hollow.

"Hey, Davey, ya big Stormer!"

She whirled round, but there was nobody there. Of course not. She had to go further up Main Street, to the gates of the school, to where she'd just remembered those immortal words.

"Where you going?" It was Hugh Cooper, the wee nutter.

"None o' your business."

"C'mon, I'll walk ye."

"Will ye hell! I'm no' walkin' doon the road wi' a wee tit like you."

His face was a picture of pain. "How no'?"

She sniffed. "Ahm waitin' for somebody."

"Who?"

"None o' your business."

"Some conversation this is turnin' out tae be."

"Nobody asked ye to start it."

"Oh, do ye prefer standing talking to yersel? Dangerous that, they say."

Where was her poise? "Don't get clever wi' me, wee man."

He grinned cheerfully. "That's me."

She glanced around, making sure that none of her friends was around to see her engaged in such an uncool activity. "Listen, what do you want?"

"You. I love ye."

She burst out laughing. "You've got to be joking! You? You?"

"That's alright, I don't expect you to love me. No' right away, anyway."

"Listen, shorty, there's no way I'd spit on you. Not now, an' no ever."

He took it calmly. "Look at it logically, Davey ..."

"Ma name's Davina!"

"... in the school you're the lassie wi' the most going for her, an' I'm the guy. It's inevitable that we'll get together."

She didn't argue with his assessment of her. "You? Whit have you got going for ye? You're a dumpling at the lessons .. ye can't play fitball, ye can't sing or play an instrument ... an' let's face it, a gorilla would gie ye a run for yer money in a beauty competition."

There was no pain this time, he stood there blinking. "That's the most words you've ever spoken tae me. I've bin counting."

"Well, it's the last an' aw. Sod off."

He was not easily daunted. "I'm going tae be an artist. I'm good at that."

He was right, something she'd missed. "Ach, you'll end up as a sign-writer."

"Mebbe. But I'm going tae give it a go. What have I got to lose?"

"You'll waste your life, you halfwit. Get a trade, get security."

"You sound like ma maw. Alright, I'll settle for a trade an' security if you'll marry me."

"You've got high hopes."

"You're only saying that cause you're taller than me."

She had to laugh at that. He stood and grinned, happy that he'd amused her. "Want to go to the swimming on Saturday?"

"No way."

"How about the pictures then?"

"No thanks. I'm already going with somebody."

"Who?"

"He's in third year. He's going to be a polis."

"He'll no' make ye happy, Davey. Never."

"Oh, ye can read people's minds now, can ye?"

120

"Whoever he is, he's not good enough for you."

"And you are?"

"I can see the future."

"It's an astrologer ye want tae be then, no' an artist."

"Do you no' believe that I love ye?"

"Was it really you drew that funny picture o' Mrs McCutcheon on the shed wall?"

"The bell rang. If I'd had more time I'd have got her moustache in as well. Do ye like me even a wee bit?"

"Gonna leave me alone."

"Wan o' these days I'm going tae paint you."

"Don't bother. I've seen the mucky drawings ye pass round the boys in the class."

"Aye. But I'd have tae do you in colour, just tae get that hair in."

"Doesn't bother me. Have you no' got a house tae go tae?"

"Just spending some time with the woman ah love. Doesn't look like yer pal's coming."

"Who said I was waiting for him?"

"C'mon, I'll walk ye home then."

She looked around. "Okay. But if anybody sees us, you're helping me cause I hurt my ankle."

"Suits me. Do ye want tae put your arm round me?"

"No chance!"

"It'd make it look more realistic. With your sore ankle and all."

"Oh aye."

"God, you smell good."

"Get your nose out of there, you wee pervert!"

"Sorry, Davey."

"Davina! Ma name's Davina! Davina .. Davina.. Davina .."

The past was hurtling away. The school railings were cold against her cheek.

"Hullo there, Davina, how's ma wee pet?"

"Hi, Mum. I'm not too bad. How are you?"

"Och, fair tae middlin'. You come visitin'?"

"Aye, Mum, thought I'd pop round."

"Ah seen aw that carry on about you in the newspapers. And ah says to myself, Davina'll be round tae see me soon for a wee chat. And here ye are. Wee Hughie Cooper eh? What a

121

rascal!"

14. GOLF AND GOD

Hugh was standing at the bar, drinking a pint. He was surrounded by the bikers and there was much hilarity and back-slapping. Bob brought over a tray of pints. "On the house, Hugh. And sorry for not serving you before, there was nothing I could do. License and all that."

Suddenly the door flew open and Fiona marched in. The bikers abandoned Hugh in a mad panic, but not before they'd each grabbed a pint from the tray. She stood with her hands on her hips, furious. "Found you at last, you two-timing philanderer. Why have you been avoiding me?"

Hugh turned slowly to face her. "You barred me from your house. You barred me from your life."

Fiona smiled warmly. "Well, I'm unbarring you."

Hugh turned back to his pint. "It's too late, Fiona. You don't destroy a man's work."

The bikers, lined against the wall, nodded in agreement.

Fiona let her lower lip tremble. "I was hurt. I thought you cared for me."

The bikers agreed with this too.

"I thought you understood me. Understood what the work meant."

This too made sense to the bikers.

Fiona let out a little sob. "I went to see her. The Stormer. She ..she .. shouted at me."

"Oh no, what did you say to her?"

"I called her a cow. I didn't know you weren't shagging her."

"Well, now you know. But it doesn't matter, because me and you are finished."

Fiona let out a loud wail. "I'm pregnant. I lost my pills."

Sympathy swung again and the bikers looked towards Hugh.

"You're not pregnant, and you never lost them. You hid them under the couch. I've been feeding you them in your cornflakes for the past six months.

Crawford, in full golfing rig, including plus fours, was out on the hotel club course, alone. He fired off a tee shot and on getting to the green, discovered that he'd holed in one. He looked around, but there were no witnesses. He shrugged and teed off again. Again, he got a hole in one, and again he looked around, but there were still no witnesses. Now, Crawford looked fearfully up to the heavens.

Various elderly members were sitting around the bar sipping drinks when Crawford arrived. He perched himself on a stool at the bar and held a drink tightly with both hands, looking grim-faced. The barman, polishing glasses behind the bar, noticed the strain on his face and came over to him. "Everything okay, sir?"

Crawford looked up slowly. "I .. I ..."

The barman nodded sympathetically. "Been one of those days, has it ? We all get them, now and again. Not to worry."

Crawford was glad of somebody to unload on. "Something very strange happened to me," he whispered, ".... started at the seventh."

"Ha, the killer seventh. That's been the downfall of many a good man. It's deceptive, see."

At a table one of the old guys started gasping and suddenly keeled over on to the floor. His friends, all concern, gathered round him, trying to help. The barman rushed out from behind the bar. He undid the old guy's tie and unbuttoned his shirt collar, but the guy started turning purple and struggling to breathe. There was a general panic, watched impassively by Crawford.

"He's having a heart attack!" the barman raged. "Is there a doctor? An ambulance ... somebody call an ambulance ..."

Now Crawford shook off his lethargy. He jumped off his stool and parted the throng with sweeping gestures. He grabbed the old man by the collar, pulled him up and gave him an almighty thump on the back. The old guy looked startled and started breathing again. Crawford dropped him to the floor and returned to his stool.

The barman returned to his station and patted Crawford's shoulder. "That was incredible. I didn't know you could fix a heart attack like that. Some people have got healing hands, you've got a healing right hook. You're a saint."

"No I'm not, I'm a police officer.   And it wasn't a heart attack, it was a peanut."

"But Mr Harrison never eats peanuts, he's allergic to them."

Crawford's face went stern again as he stared at the barman.

Hugh was showing Davina round the Kelvingrove art gallery, pointing out favourite pictures, trying to infect her with his enthusiasm. "Rembrandt's Guy in Armour, now that's a masterpiece."

"He looks constipated."

"The Madonna and Child with the infant St John, that's by Pesellino."

"Don't like it."

"And this Madonna and Child is by Bellini."

"That kid doesn't look well."

"Okay, how about The Adulteress brought before Christ by Titian?   Check the colours."

"Forgive her, Lord."

" This is The Blute-Fin Windmill, by Van Gogh."

"Anthony Quinn."

"No, he was Gaugin.   Kirk Douglas played Van Gogh."

He raced along, dragging her behind him.   Held her the correct viewing distance from differently sized paintings, mimed the brush strokes required for a particular section, but it was obvious that her mind was elsewhere.   She stopped him suddenly and made a telling statement, "Just remember, Hugh Cooper, girls can have Stormers too."

"Which says I'm not yours."

"I never said that."

"You didn't have to.   I know it doesn't have to be a two-way street."

"What if you *were* my Stormer?"

"I'd need to have you seen to.   Look at the state of me."

"I thought the title didn't just go with looks."

"They help."

"So I can be your Stormer, but you can't be mine."

"Not in a sane world."

"You're a tough deal, Cooper."

"I know."

At the park where they'd jogged Hugh and Davina walked together. Davina was in shorts and seemed as frisky as a teenager. She was trying to trip Hugh up. They came to a clump of bushes and Davina tried to drag him into them, but he fought her off.

"You can't still be shy at your age," she complained, "Why, your fiancee claimed you shagged her bandy when you first met."

"She's not my fiancee, never was. We were just, well, good for each other for a while."

Davina realised he was serious. "And you stopped being good for each other?"

"I always thought of relationships as being like the Cold War. Two power blocs shoving away at each other. Well, I'm Russia, I quit."

"So, now you're rebuilding?"

"No, now I'm confused."

"That makes two of us."

Hugh gave a wan smile. "It doesn't help, seeing you."

Davina gave him a hard stare. "Well why don't you just bugger off. I'm not the one who painted you in the buff. I'm not the one who came crashing into your life."

"That's not what I mean. Just, seeing you again, after all these years is ......"

"Destiny?"

"Maybe. All I know is that when I'm with you I'm a stupid boy again; gawky, struck dumb. But, still bursting with hormones."

"What's stopping you then, kid ? I'm up for it, I've told you."

"Naah, that was a sweet sixteen year old I fancied. I don't want an old broad like you."

She dropped her chin and her lip trembled. Hugh, regretful, moved forward to comfort her, only to be slapped across the head by her handbag. He ran and she chased him, flailing at him with her bag.

That night they were in her dining room and Hugh was sitting at the well set-out table. Davina was working in the adjoining kitchen.

Hugh looked at the wedding photograph on the wall, with a radiant Davina and a hairier Crawford. "I feel incredibly uncomfortable."

Davina brought through a steaming casserole. She was dressed much more to suit her age in a shortish skirt and singlet top. She was also wearing a little make-up and altogether looked quite stunning.

"Don't worry, I'm not going to drag you off to bed till after dinner."

"Don't say bed, it makes me horny."

"Bed, bed, bed, bed, bed, bed." She stuck out her tongue at him and he shook his head, worried at the monster he'd unleashed.

Midden was working on his bike when his sister drove up in her car and stood over him.

"What am I supposed to do with him?" she demanded loudly. "He's a lunatic. Am I a bad woman ? Have I ever let him down ? Didn't I support him ? Fed him, watered him, satisfied his carnal desires ....."

Midden slowly stood up. "Listen, Feef, you're my sister, and I love you. But Hugh ... well, Hugh's special .... you know that."

"Of course, I know, that's why I want him back."

"You shouldn't have ripped up his paintings. There was a lot of blood and graft went into them."

"I lost the rag, I admit it."

"Thing with Hugh is, he never gave up, and people loved him for it. Every painting he did, year after year, every rejection, every insult, Hugh came bouncing back. He had a talent, he knew it, and he was going to prove it."

Fiona made a disgusted face. "Oh my, my, you'll be starting a fan club for the wee soul next."

Midden smiled. "He was just a wounded sparrow to you. Something to mother. But you've done your job, it's time to let him go."

"Very poetic. And I get nothing for all the time and effort I put in to making him what he is?"

"You should be happy just to see him fly."

"He's not flying with any red-headed floozy, that's for sure. I don't suppose there's any chance of you and the boys cutting his baws off with a rusty knife?"

Midden looked at her sadly and shook his head. She walked back to her car and shouted back at him as she climbed in. "Outlaw bikers, by god! I'd be better off getting a bunch of hari krishnas and filling them full of cheap wine !"

Hugh and Davina sat at a café table, sipping cappuccinos. The autumn had relented to a warm evening and she was wearing a hat and brightly coloured summer frock. "Crawford's due back tomorrow," she said.

Hugh smiled. "Well, it couldn't last forever."

"Why not?"

"It would never work, Davey. You're too much the middle class housewife now, and I'm still the fucked-up starving artist. You're not wild enough for my world and I'm not straight enough for yours."

"For you, dear sir, I'd learn fire-walking, hedgehog juggling and advanced accountancy. How wild do you want me?"

"Old dogs and new tricks, unfortunately, can't be done. We could both have fun in each others' worlds for a while, but eventually I'd hear the call of the wild, and you'd hear the call of the quiche."

She suddenly reached across and stroked his face. "Okay," she said, wrinkling her nose, "Once, let's just do it once."

He pulled away from her sharply. "No ! There's nothing like reality for killing a dream. Let's leave each other that."

"The Stormer was the dream. I'm real."

"Too real. Too dangerous."

"Yeah. So why paint 'The Stormer' ?"

He slumped. "There's a Stormer in every man's life, Davey. All the woman he can hope for. All the love, friendship, hope, companionship, and unfettered fornication he can ever imagine. You were mine."

She lifted a knife from the table and pointed it at his throat. "You bastard!" she hissed.

He pulled back from her. "Hey! What's up?"

Her snarl turned to a grin. "You made my nipples hard."

The finished their coffee and left the cafe. Davina took his arm. "Even when Crawford's back, we can still see each other now and again."

"I don't think so, why keep tormenting each other ? Let's just take this as the platonic holiday fling it was."

"That's easy for you to say, you're in a life you enjoy."

"A life I'm driven to."

"Let me in, Hugh, please."

"Why ? What can I give you ? One painting doesn't make a career."

"You're determined to make me suffer for a decision I made as a child. People change, Hugh. I've changed."

Hugh nodded, looked around. "Yeah, but will you still love me when I'm dead and gone?"

Davina cocked her head, wondering how serious he was. "Planning something spectacular ?"

"No, just there's Fiona across the road, and I'm sure she wants to kill me."

Across the road, Fiona was sitting in her car, watching them through binoculars. She lowered the glasses and nodded, satisfied that she'd uncovered some sordid truth..

15. SALVATION

Davina drove home and entered the lounge to find Crawford sitting in an armchair, reading a Bible.

"I'm back early, and I've surprised you," he said calmly, "You've been with him, haven't you ? You've been in the arms of he who uncovered your nakedness."

She threw her bag on the couch and started peeling off her jacket. "Crawford? Finally flipped?"

"The Lord moves in mysterious ways, Davina. I have had many signs during my time in the wilderness."

"Wilderness ? I thought you were golfing."

"A figure of speech. It is common practice for the chosen one to go into seclusion, away from his normal abode, to receive divine revelation."

Davina slumped into the armchair opposite him. "We need to talk."

"No. It is a time for listening. I have been too lenient with you, Davina. I have allowed you to mix with evil beings, bad elements, those that are destined for the wrath divine. But this must end. The Lord has spoken. I can take no more."

He stood up with the Bible in one hand and tried to lay his hand on Davina's head in a blessing. She pushed him away.

"Me too, Mr Gillespie. Reach for your lawyer."

Burroughs spluttered as he read the hand-written letter. Finally, finished, he looked up at Crawford. "Resigning to join the ministry?"

"I've had the call, sir, I cannot refuse the Lord."

Burroughs stood up and came round from his desk to puts his arm round Crawford's shoulders. "Too many church parades, Crawford, that's all. They've nothing to do with religion, you know."

"I'm speaking at the morality rally in the Civic Hall next week. I'd be very honoured if you could come along."

Burroughs patronisingly led him towards the door. "Yes, Crawford, of course I'll be there. I'll bring the boys from Vice and Narcotics with me, they enjoy a good sermon."

Hugh was standing in the porch as Davina answered the door. She smiled and stood aside to let him in.

"I'm not coming in," Hugh said.

"He's not here. You're quite safe."

"It's not that."

"He's staying with friends. We're getting divorced."

"I heard."

"So it's quite safe for you to come in and ravish me to your heart's content."

"It's not that, Davey. This doesn't change anything."

"I'm a free woman. You're a free man. We love each other .... as far as I know."

Hugh tried to explain but knew that he didn't have the words. "I just don't want to get it wrong. Let anybody down. It's got to be right. Perfect."

She leaned over and kissed his cheek. "Listen, Coop, nothing is ever totally right, totally perfect. That's for movies and fairy stories. In real life we screw up, we make mistakes, we keep going."

"Every cell in my body is screaming for me to go inside with you."

Davina stood back, smiling. "Come in, cells."

But Hugh demurred. "And I know it's wrong. I've spent so much time getting to this moment that I'm not going to blow it now. Maybe I'm not your answer. Maybe I'm just a key that opens the door to your future."

She leaned down and kissed him on the lips. She started off comforting but lips locked and they moved closer to each other. He drank her in. His hands crept round her waist and pulled her towards him. His hands slipped down and squeezed, and despite the ambitions this fulfilled he pulled away.

"No! I need time."

Davina felt cheated. "As long as it's not twenty years."

Hugh nodded and turned to walk away down the path. Davina watched him go, a faint quiver on her lips.

She needed to talk and made her way over to Audrey's house. Audrey's house was much like Davina's, only Audrey had sub-teen children and evidence of their existence was everywhere. Davina trailed Audrey round the house as she tidied up.

Audrey couldn't help but be judgmental. "I could see this coming, of course, the minute you started carrying on with that painter."

"I was not carrying on with him. Well, just a little flirting. Anyway, I was thinking of leaving Crawford long before all this happened. We'd just become two strangers living together."

"I'm going to tell you exactly the same as your mother did. You should have had kids."

Davina had heard this all before and had a set of pat answers. She reeled them of now. "Oh, I know, but there was Crawford's career. He wanted to wait. Use what money we had to make an impression socially. Till he got well on his way up the ladder."

"Oh, pish, Davina. I can tell a man with a low sperm count just by looking at him. I suppose you're free to fly into your painter's arms now."

"I don't think he wants me."

Audrey paused with what she was doing and gave her friend a hard glare. "Doesn't want you? Don't be stupid."

"He thinks we're too different. Him being an artist and me being ... well, nothing."

Audrey stopped dead and threw all the toys she'd been picking up on to the ground. She grabbed Davina's shoulders. "Listen, girl, why are you so determined to demean yourself?" She let Davina go but started stabbing a finger at her. "You? Nothing? You?" 'Nothing' doesn't inspire people to great art, you daft bitch. If a man made that kind of statement for me, I'd have my legs round him so tight you couldn't get me off with a crowbar and vaseline."

The image made Davina laugh which pleased Audrey. "I'd pay to see that, Audrey, I can just see you. Six firemen toiling to get you off some poor man."

Audrey narrowed her eyes. "Oooh, six firemen!"

"How can you be such a slut and a happily married woman at the same time?"

"Oh come on, you know I only talk slut."

Davina came on her daily visit to look at The Stormer and ended up standing next to The Shame. He'd seen her many times before but had never been able to muster the courage to speak to her. Now he cautiously cleared his throat and she turned to look at him.

"You must be a big fan," she said, "I see you here every time I come."

"I'm the official guardian of The Stormer. Shame's the name."

She smiled and made his day. "You're the one who's been looking after Hugh, aren't you? You're doing too good a job, he's putting on weight."

"Just passing on the survival skills I learned on the streets."

"Still, you've kept him alive and I thank you for that."

"My pleasure. It's an honour to guard the painting, and to see you every day, for you are to be a work of art yourself."

"You are very gallant, sir."

"I have been in my day, my lady, but you find me at my nadir."

She said, "Your penance is over, I so will it," and immediately wondered why she'd made such an outrageously hopeful judgment.

"A blessing from thee is as gold."

She glanced at her watch. "Would you care to join me for some lunch?"

He gave her his best bashful look. "Apologies, my Stormer, my raiment is not suitable to accompany thee to all but the most humble of premises."

"Then we shall adjourn there. I see a diner of the lowest type across yonder road. Would that suit thee?"

"Indeed, for their broth is as ambrosia and I have supped their often." He stretched out an arm, inviting her to lead him, but instead she took his arm and together they crossed the street to the diner.

The waitress, who had served Shame often, was stunned. She looked at Davina as she took a seat and stared out of the window at the painting. She hurried over and asked, "Excuse me, are you …?" and she pointed.

Davina nodded nervously and Shame came to her aid like any good knight. "This lady is my guest and should be treated as such, young Jean. Now, fetch us a menu so we may peruse your comestibles."

"Tell me about yourself," Davina requested as they finally sat eating their soup.

"There is not much to tell, my lady, and surely not fitting for ears such as yours."

"Perhaps, but thou shall know a man by his comrades, their variety and their deeds. Speak on."

"In truth, in my younger days, I was something of a go-getter, but I woke one morning to find that my get-up-and-go had got-up-and-gone. And that is how you find me thus. And je ne regrette rien too, by the way."

"And wast thou ever wed?"

He nodded. "To Mary, a bonny lass, of blonde coiffure and full of silly notions. She left me for another man."

"Alas."

"Not so. She had not in her that quality of giving herself to one man. This man she left me for will have discovered that when she left him bereft."

"Of such poor substance are we made. Of error and confusion."

"I bore the pain as men have ever done."

"And women too, sire! I shall not have thee claim all virtue for thy gender."

"My apologies, twas but a slip of the tongue, I meant no offence."

"And thou hast not loved since?"

"The road is a poor place for romantic encounter and my current garb, my very countenance, would scarce encourage it."

"You do yourself a disservice, sirrah."

"But nay, do not flatter me. I know that which I am. I am a man of the road, no home, no job, no hopes. These are not the attributes which catch the eyes of maidens."

"And yet you stand and guard The Stormer."

"It was asked of me by an honest man and I could not refuse him."

"You think him honest then?"

The Shame lowered his head. "Dost thou jest?"

"Nay, I seek only the truth."

But their conversation was interrupted by Jean who cleared their soup plates and brought them pie, chips and beans. She also asked for an autograph but Davina insisted that the Shame signed first, so that she could add, Guardian of The Stormer, below it.

"You doubt then your knight's intent?" The Shame asked once Jean had retreated.

"He withholds his intent from me and that must give me pause."

"Perhaps he himself has not established it."

"His timing is fraught then. He claims a declaration on yonder wall, but says nothing of what his declaration is."

"Yet he is a good knight, a kind knight. If he fails thee it is not for any lack in his heart, tis because he is a knight and must set high ideals."

"Such things are for godlings and we are mere mortals not worthy of perfection."

"We may not be worthy of achieving it, but we are worthy of seeking it."

"I tire of his searching."

"All things pass, lady. Have patience, thy time will come."

"You too are a good knight, Sir Shame."

"Old, lady, old. My jousting days are behind me. Now I lie under a starless sky and there are no dreams."

She reached across and stroked his hand. "Come, sir, I shall not have thy depression. Think on the days before thou met Sir Hugh. Hast thou not purpose now, hast thou not drive, does every day not bring promise of adventure?"

"Oh yes," The Shame cried, "I live again and it is joy. For that I thank thee."

"Not I."

"Nay? If it were not my lady's image on that wall what purpose would I serve?"

"From a distance then I'll take some measure of the credit for thy renaissance."

The Shame looked suddenly worried. "I fear its passing, lady. What shall become of thy servant then?"

"Thou shall fly, Sir Shame, for having met thee I cannot let you fall again. I so vow." And having said that she finished her last chip and called for coffee.

Midden drove up to the Dog's Breath with Hugh on the pillion. They dismounted and walked towards the door.

"She never said a word after that," Midden told his friend, "the Feef, just disappeared. That's when she's at her most dangerous. She was six years old when she shot my dog."

They entered the bar and walked over to their usual company.

"She's up to something," Midden continued, "I'm telling you. Be careful. They threw her out of the SS for cruelty."

Hugh appreciated the attempt at uplift but wasn't in the mood. "I didn't mean to hurt her, Midden, honest, I didn't mean to hurt anybody. But my head's so mixed up. The Stormer was just a painting, meant nothing, but then ....."

"That's the trouble with you bloody artists. You can't be like ordinary folk and just say - I love you, get them off."

"I was well brought up, Midden, you know that, I always say please."

"Aye, you've got this weird notion that sex has got something to do with love."

"Clean underpants every day, that's how romantic I can be."

"You don't even know this lassie, never jumped her bones or anything. What kind of basis is that for a relationship?"

"I told you before, Midden, don't do sensible."

"Has anybody seen Fiona?" Midden asked the bikers.

As ones who know the meaning of fear the bikers turned away from the pair and went into a defensive huddle.

At the gable end wall Shame was standing in front of the mural, lecturing to a group of foreign tourists. "The Stormer is, of course, Mr Cooper's masterwork and he admits himself that he was influenced by many great artists that have gone before him.   He owes a debt to Bottle O'Chilli, for instance, and if you look at her out of the side of your eye, you can see that him and that Lenny Da Vinci have had a few beers together. Notice how her nipples follow you, wherever you go, that's genius, that is."

He passed his cap round and the tourists reluctantly started putting money in.   Hugh came strolling along and Shame swiftly pocketed the money and put the cap back on his head. He scurried over to Hugh. "Alright, chief?   No problems here.   Your girl is as safe as houses."

Hugh nodded and looked up at The Stormer.

"Could you just sign these bits of paper, it's those tourists, you know what they're like."

Shame shoved his notebook and a pen into Hugh's hand and flicked over the pages as Hugh absentmindedly signed them. Hugh concentrated on the mural again, whistling to himself. Shame chased after the tourists and with a lot of visual haggling he offered the autographs while pointing back at Hugh. "Himself.   I'm telling you. The man."

Having done various nefarious deals the Shame returned to stand beside Hugh.

"She comes every day, you know," he said.

"Who ?

Shame nodded towards the mural. "Herself.   She comes to check how she's keeping, I suppose."

Hugh snapped out of it and looked at Shame directly for the first time. "Are there people here when she comes?   The public?"

"Oh aye, there's always people here."

"And they know it's her?"

"Couldn't be anybody else."

"So who do they look at most, her or the painting?"

Shame's eyes darted about as he considered the correct response to this.   He tugged at his nose, cleared his throat. "Both!   They look at them both.   Equally.   I've timed them."

Hugh burst out laughing.   He pulled cash from his pocket and tucked some notes into Shame's coat.

"The danger should be passed now but keep your eyes open, just in case.   You're doing a great job." Hugh turned to walk away, but then returned to the Shame.

"Does she ever say anything?" he asked the tramp. He looked up at the mural.

The Shame smiled, displaying his snaggled, tobacco stained teeth. "No, but she gets through a lot of paper hankies."

"I'd appreciate it if you could bring the PAP group round," Crawford said to Archie on the phone.

"Ah, thing is, membership's gone down a bit since you left, Colin."

"My name's really Crawford," the ex-policeman replied, glad to shrug of the shackles of an alias now that he was beginning a new life. "How many members have you got now?"

"Just me and the lady wife. Back to basics."

"I'd still be glad to see you. You're the kind of people I need in my new ministry."

"I'm very impressed, Colin .. Crawford. You've taken all my plans up to an entirely higher level. But then you've got it, haven't you. The old charisma."

"If it takes charisma to gather followers I'll get it. So you'll come?"

"Wouldn't miss it for the world. It's positively exciting to be in on the start of something new."

In the Civic Hall that night Crawford made his debut as a preacher. His audience consisted mainly of old, grumpy-looking women. Other speakers, seated behind him, were vicar-types with the grim visages of Old Testament prophets.

Crawford wanted to make an immediate impact, so he started with, "Lewdness and nudity. These are the cancers that gnaw at our vitals in this new age of Sodom. We are surrounded by women who think nothing of flaunting their nakedness in the faces of the godly."

Everybody nodded solemnly in agreement, knowing that this night was likely to knock an evening in front of the telly into a cocked hat.

There is suicide and there is murder. Hugh felt self-bereaved.

To think, he'd been that close. He'd actually kissed her. After all these years, full-bodied, no holds barred, everything. 'Your father had to marry me after kissing me like that.'

He'd felt her arse. These grubby paint-ingrained hands had squeezed the bum of the most beautiful woman in the world. All those adolescent fantasies, that sweet ass. And that memory of delightful tension would linger on his hand, to be remembered when he was old and totally degenerate.

And he'd let it go.

Jeeze god, it's no' fair. All my life, all my life, for what? I'd give it all up, I would. I would. Wouldn't I?

And there could be no more dreams of maybe now, she wouldn't need him.

The Stormer was strong.

And you chased her away, Hugh Cooper, don't forget that. She was practically throwing herself at you. Every erotic notion fulfilled, every inspiration you could ever desire, something solid in your life at last.

But not you, shit head, you had to put her to the test. You had to pretend you didn't love her. Make her think she didn't love you.

And did she? Did she?

You were the key, Hugh, you were the key. Fine state of

affairs for a grown man.   And what do you do for a living?
I'm a key.
Accept defeat. Lay down your arms. Grieve for the dead and
rest your weary bones.   What's it all about, God?

Rita Writes:
A World Exclusive for you this week and I make no excuses
for devoting my entire column to an interview with Davina
Gillespie (nee McLean).
Who? You may well ask.   For Davina is no superstar, no
model, no actress, no pop singer, but her face is as well known
across this city as any of the glitterati.   Davina is, in fact, an
ordinary Glaswegian housewife, who cooks her man's dinner,
manages a white wash twice a week and does the grocery
shopping on Saturday mornings.   But, and this is important,
she is also the person that inspired The Stormer, that stunning
mural in the city's west end. Note that I do not say that Davina
is The Stormer, for this is something Davina insists upon. As
she says, "The Stormer is a painting and I am a human being."
So, why did I track down this wife of a Superintendent of
Strathclyde Police to her leafy home in Bearsden?   Two
reasons. One, I had previously commented on the burdens of
being so improbably beautiful and was desperate to meet
someone who was.   And two, Davina and I share the
distinction of having both been painted by Hugh Cooper.
Please also remember that I instigated this pursuit, for Davina
has no interest in fame and is rather embarrassed by the furore
the mural has caused. But, having given you so much on Hugh
Cooper, it seemed only fair that I allowed you to meet the
woman who was his inspiration.   I report the conversation
verbatim and have asked my editor not to illustrate this piece
with any distracting photographs. If there is a photograph of
The Stormer sitting beside this column it means he has ignored
my wishes and shall be removed from my Christmas card list.
(As if I'd dare. Ed.)

RR:Davina, when did you first learn of The Stormer?

DG:The same time as everybody else, I suppose. I saw a picture of the mural in a newspaper and everybody commented on how much it resembled me.

RR:And what was your reaction?

DG:I don't know. It's hard to define. There's pleasure that somebody, somewhere, has acknowledged your existence, and there's a certain annoyance that they've somehow intruded on you. It's a strange mixture of feelings.

RR:I assume you've been to see the mural. Do you like it?

DG:I love it, but not because it's supposed to be me. I love it because it's a great piece of art.

RR:So, you're not offended by the nudity?

DG:(Laughs) I've seen myself naked.

RR:But as a private citizen you must have had some qualms about being portrayed in this fashion.

DG:Not really. As I keep saying, that painting is not me. To appear naked myself would be mortifying, but that's just paint.

RR: Would you have posed for it if asked?

DG: I'm a wee lassie from the east end of Glasgow, we don't do stuff like that.

RR:And your husband's reaction.

DG:I'd rather not discuss that. Let's just say that he wasn't as open-minded as me about it.

RR:Now, I wrote in a previous column about the burdens that beauty places on the bearer, and you are undoubtedly a beautiful woman. Is that a pain?

DG:Beauty is a judgment other people make. My features are a certain way, and other people's are different. Who's to judge what's beauty? I'm certainly not qualified.

RR:Oh, come now, you must know that you're beautiful.

DG:I've had this face all my life. I've gone from being a bonny baby, to a good looking girl, to a beautiful woman, or so people tell me. I'm not in a business where beauty counts. The housewife business requires ironed shirts in the morning, not stunning beauty. Actresses and models might find things different, for them beauty is a tool, for me it's just a fact of life.

RR:But your looks make you the envy of thousands if not millions.

DG: Ah, I'd dispute that. From everyone I've spoken to it's not my looks that people are jealous of, but the fact that the artist retained such affection for me for so long.

RR: Yes, the talented Mr Cooper. Did you remember him from your schooldays?

DG: Only vaguely.

RR: Well, you're in danger of losing your fan club there. Everybody hoped that a love that remained so long would be reciprocated.

DG: Well, that would be difficult as I'm a married woman. But I'd just like to make this clear. Hugh was attracted to me when we were younger, but I never returned those feelings. He didn't loom large in my life.

RR: This is what I find so confusing. As you know I've met Hugh and I think I know him. He doesn't seem the type that wouldn't have let you know that he was attracted to you.

DG: Oh, he told me, a lot. But the schoolboy Hugh was not the Hugh of today. What he offered as a potential partner was not what I was looking for.

RR: Which was?

DG: Mrs Reynolds, I was brought up in a two room tenement flat in Bridgeton and my parents taught me that the most important thing in a girl's life was to seek security through a good marriage.

RR: That seems incredibly old-fashioned.

DG: You may think so, and maybe things are different nowadays with the career opportunities that are open to women. But in my day, unless a girl was driven to something, to some profession, she had to look after number one, herself. I know that makes me sound terribly cold and selfish, but it was the reality we had to deal with. I had no particular talents I could bring to the job market and could only better myself by marrying a man with prospects.

RR: You had your looks.

DG: And nobody knew them until Hugh Cooper put them on a wall. It's taken me just as long to be discovered as it has Hugh. But Hugh can paint for the next fifty years and my looks are already starting to fade.

RR:Are you grateful to Hugh, or rather, that's the wrong question, what are your feelings towards Hugh now?

DG:It's that same mixture I had before, Rita. Confusion, mainly. There is a feeling of someone having intruded into my life, but there's also pleasure at an essentially mundane life being enhanced.

RR:So what are the differences between the schoolboy and the artist?

DG:Man and boy? It's hard to say because I hardly knew the boy and I'm only slowly getting to know the man. He was good at drawing at school, I knew that. He was a cheeky item, I knew that.

RR:(Laughs) And still is.

DG:But that's exactly it. He's still so much the boy and I think he still holds those feelings for me. But I'm different. I'm grown. I'm married. So, I think it's unfair of him, or anybody else for that matter, to see this as some kind of a fairy tale with a happy ending.

RR:But there are rumours that you and your husband have separated.

DG:That's an entirely separate issue and not one I'm prepared to discuss in public.

RR:Are you honestly trying to tell me that The Stormer had nothing to do with the break down of your marriage?

DG:No, that would be foolish. The Stormer was a factor in precipitating the events that have led to my current situation, but I am still a married woman and I am not going to disparage my husband here.

RR:For a housewife you're a very able politician.

DG:I'm not trying to be deliberately evasive, it's just that I don't know how things are going to pan out, so it would be foolish to make predictions.

RR:Did you ever have any inkling about The Stormer?

DG:None. What we have is a sequence of events that nobody could have expected. My husband and I had the opportunity to move to Australia several year ago. If we'd taken it I probably would never have heard of The Stormer. And the other side of the coin is that Hugh had no idea of who I was and where I was so, to that extent, I came crashing back into his life and intruded. He had a life and relationships before he did that painting and where are they now?

RR:Where indeed?

DG:You'll have to ask Hugh that.

RR:Do you see any future for yourself as a model?

DG:Hardly. For one thing, as I've said, my age is against me, and for another it's a helluva challenge to a painter to top The Stormer.

RR:I was thinking more of a photographic or fashion model. Or perhaps endorsing products. You have a well kent face now Do you see any future in that world?

DG:As I said, I don't know where my future lies. But I don't have any particular interest in selling myself or anything else.

RR:Make-up manufacturers would be willing to pay you fortunes for your stamp of approval.

DG:No, I'd draw the line there. I can't tell lies. If you want to look like me, girls, you have to get my Mum and Dad to be your parents

RR:(Laughs)

DG:Leave me some dignity, Rita.

RR:What do you think of the painting Hugh did of me?

DG:He should have called it The Stormer, Later.

RR:Ah, now I really see the beauty that Hugh saw in you. Thank you, Davina.

16. ENDGAME

Fiona drove up to the wall and took several plastic carrier bags from the boot and placed them carefully at her feet. She stood in front of the mural, looking up, hands on hips.

Finally she bent down and started pulling empty bottles from one of the carrier bag. She lined them up in front of her, took a can of petrol from another bag and started filling the bottles.

Shame was on his bench, covered by his Chinese newspaper, snoring. He woke now, sniffed the air and licked his lips. He looked round, saw Fiona and what she was doing, and jumped to his feet startled.

"Hey!" he shouted, "What are you doing, young madam?"

"Fuck off," Fiona replied.

The Shame sniffed again. "Is that petrol?"

"Naw, it's eau de cologne, now fuck off and leave me alone."
Shame approached her tentatively. "It is, it's petrol. What are you up to?"
"You can call it petrol, I call it revenge juice."
"I am entrusted by the artist, Mr Hugh Cooper with defending his painting. Don't you go near it."
"Oh, you know Hugh, do you? Well, you tell him it was Fiona Ferguson that burnt down his fucking lovely Stormer. I don't want him thinking it was an act of God or anything."
Shame stopped dead in his tracks. "Burn it? Are you mad, woman?"
"No, I'm just crazy."
"You can't burn The Stormer."
"Oh yes I can."
And she continued filling the bottles and the Shame didn't know how to react. Finally he pointed a finger at her. "I'll have to stop you. It's my duty."
"You and whose army?"
The Shame saw a strategy. Fiona was lining up the bottles in straight lines in front of her. If he ran up and kicked them, they would smash and she would be thwarted. It seemed sensible, but the Shame had never even attempted a run in over twenty years and his body had forgotten how. He took two awkward steps, lost his balance and fell over on his face.
"Aye," Fiona gloated, "Guard his painting? That Hugh knows how to pick his staff."
The Shame thought he'd lost the ability to feel embarrassed, but as he clambered to his feet, his face burned.
"Stop what you're doing right now," he bellowed, "I'm warning you."
"Away and drink out of a sewer, ya manky old bastard." Fiona turned towards him, took two quick steps forward and kicked him firmly in the groin. It had no effect, the Shame after years of alcohol abuse and abstinence, was beyond pain. Her move had brought her closer however and he stumbled forward and grabbed her by the shoulders. "Right, you witch."
But all he'd grabbed was her jacket. She wriggled out of it, lifted one of the bottles and crashed it down on the Shame's balding skull. Despite the lack of pain, he crumpled to his

knees. Fiona searched frantically for matches or some other means of ignition to complete her plan, but found nothing. She dashed back to her car.

Meanwhile Crawford was still working his audience. "And does the Bible itself not say, in Genesis, Chapter 3, Verse 7 - 'And the eyes of them both were opened, and they knew that they were naked; and they sewed fig leaves together, and made themselves aprons'.
Aprons, ladies and gentlemen ... 'they sewed together fig leaves and made themselves ... aprons'. And we .. we with our superstores, our shops, our malls, our fashion boutiques, what fig leaves shall we not sew into aprons?"

Shame stood up, in a panic, unsure of what to do. He took a few paces in one direction, then a feeble sprint in the other. His body slowly remembered how to run. He saw a phone box and ran towards it. Once inside he gingerly lifted the receiver, and held it to his ear, but working it was beyond him.
"Hugh? Are you there?" he shouted. Receiving no answer but a dialling tone he threw the receiver away from him and dashed rapidly off into the night.

Crawford had the old ladies up to a high pitch of excitement. "The voice of morality must be heard once more across the nation. No more nudity! No more nakedness! Ban the bare!"
The audience rose to their feet, shouting, chanting, braying, but weakly, "Ban the Bare! Ban the Bare!"
Placards, conveniently supplied by Archie, were produced reading 'Down With the Stormer'.
Crawford leapt from the stage and led his geriatric army through the door. A policeman, expecting a quiet night, was standing at the door but they brushed him aside. He spotted their leader and the placards and reached for his radio.

In police headquarters Sgt Watt was on the phone. "Nuts, Mrs Gillespie, the Chief reckons he's gone a bit nuts. Perhaps if you could come down, have a word, we'd rather not arrest him.

Davina put the phone down and slumped into an armchair. Audrey sitting across from her, sipped from a glass of wine. "Problem?" she asked.

"It's Crawford. It seems he's leading a band of crazed old women over to sort out the painting."

Audrey sniffed. "Well, at least he's with his own kind."

"The cops want me to go down and talk to him," Davina said. "So they don't have to arrest him." She made to stand up.

"He's not your responsibility any more. Don't fall into the trap of feeling sorry for him and going running every time he's got a runny nose."

Davina slid back.

Finally she stood. "He was ... is .. my husband."

"Bugger him, he's a fruit bat. Here, pour me some more loony juice."

Davina considered for a moment and then lifted a set of car keys from the table.

"Hey, those are mine," Audrey said.

"I have to go, and your car's faster."

Audrey smiled superior. "You'll never be able to handle it."

"I know, that's why you'll have to stop drinking and come with me."

Audrey shrugged, stood up and took the keys. "You still care for him that much?"

"It's not him I'm trying to save."

In the Dog's Breath, Midden, came over to Hugh, grabbed his wrist, and whispered, "The meeting's tonight."

"Oh aye, what one's that?"

"Don't come it. Inaugural meeting. We're finally getting started."

Hugh prised Midden's fingers from his wrist. "Haven't a clue what you're talking about, Midden."

"See you, Hugh, ye can be a right wee neb. The hammer an' the saltire, mind we talked about it. The political party we're forming. Scottish Socialism."

Layers of sodden memory peeled away. "We were drunk, Midden. We were drunk."

Midden gestured that aside. "It was you, Hugh. You were the

one that came up with the idea. You were the one that came up with the name. We're just providing the manpower but you're providing the brains."

Another biker, Mixer, piped up with, "What brains?"

Don't start, Mixer." Midden snapped, "We know you're an expert, but you can't get the boys falling out with one another. We know ye."

"He's right but," Hugh said, "I've not got the brains for politics."

Midden was affronted. "But you came up with the idea. The name!"

"Scotialism? You think that's good?"

"A cracker! The very dab! You've got a mind on ye like a Maserati, Hugh. Ye were right. Labour's finished. The Tories were never in it. The SNP have shot their wad, an' the Liberal Democrats is all poofs. Scotland's crying out for Scotialism."

"They'll need a damn big hanky then, Hugh said. He stubbed out his cigarette, pushed back his stool and stood up. "I'll come to your meeting, but just for a laugh."

"He's gone power mad," Mixer said emphatically.

"Zatafact."

"It's true. Midden's gone off his chump."

"Mixer, don't do it.' Don't try an' mix it with *us*. We know ye could start a war in an ashram, but don't try an' mix it with the boys."

"Would you listen, that Scotialism of yours has gone right to Midden's head. And I'm not mixing it, honest, ask anybody. That Scotialism, straight to his head. Now he wants to be King."

"King?"

Mixer nodded, his granny glasses flashing in the bar's dim red light. "King of Scotland," he said emphatically.

Hugh shrugged and drank his beer. "Fair enough."

Mixer replied with a highly dramatic startled expression. "Scotialism. You said. A republic."

Hugh had tried for so long to break Mixer from his habit of talking in individual portions that he was beyond annoyance. "I never said no such thing. You're mixing it."

"Am not."

"You are. Ye know it. Stop it." God, I'm doing it myself now.

Mixer grinned. "Ah, fair enough. But do ye want Midden for King?"

Hugh swallowed the dregs of the beer and set his glass down. "I want you out of my face. If we ever do get independence for this country, you're not getting the job of foreign minister, that's for sure. Christ, you'd have us at war before we'd got the stamps printed."

Mixer nodded his thanks at the compliment and followed Hugh through to the lounge.

Several of the brass-topped tables had been pushed together to form an alcoholics' committee room. Between the brimming glasses and ashtrays lay sheaves of typewritten pages. Hugh sat down, glanced at the SCOTIALISM title and the crudely drawn Hammer & Saltire logo he'd once swiftly sketched on a bar mat and pushed the offending sheets away.

"Listen, I can take a joke, boys ..." he started.

Midden glanced up from some important document. "Meeting's not come to order yet, Mr Cooper," he conveyed, more in the tone of a trade union delegate than a potential monarch.

Hugh shrugged and glanced round the company.

"All right, boys?"

They all looked up at him in disapproval. He smiled happily then turned and jabbed a finger towards Midden. "What's this I hear about you wanting to be King ?"

Midden, usually pale, went two shades lighter. "Ah was going to make you a Duke, Hugh," he explained.

Is that higher than a count?" Mixer wanted to know, "You said I could be a count."

"Are you sure it wasn't 'cunt'?"

"Who said that?"

Midden rapped his fist on the table, spilling no little beer. "Monarchy of the Masses, it's a step to Dictatorship o' the Proletariat. Everybody knows that."

Hugh grunted. "You make up your Marx as you go along, same as everybody else. Scotialism, that's what we're fighting for. Socialism for the Scottish people, and tailored to their

147

needs. And apart from that, ah don't even believe in it any more."

They all went silent. Eventually Midden creased his brow and asked, "What?"

"If we get independence and form a government we'll have to move to Edinburgh. That's the capital. Think on that."

They turned to look at each other, murmuring assent and nodding.

"What do you propose, Hugh?" Mixer asked.

"The city state of Glasgow," Hugh said proudly.

The thought rocked them, their eyes bulged.

You think about it, " Hugh ordered, " And we'll talk about it later. Have a wee meeting."

Just then, the Shame came barrelling in through the door, out of breath from running.

"Hugh boy, she's there," he shouted, "the blonde you warned me about. And she's got ... she's got ... intercontinental ballistic milk bottles!"

Hugh, Midden and the bikers bolted for the door and their bikes.

They raced through the streets of Glasgow, a motley collection of chopped motorbikes, half-chopped motorbikes, motorbikes that were going to be chopped, motorbikes with sidecars and a couple of trikes because some of the guys liked to do the shopping for their missus.

An avenging army, a posse, a group of outlaw bikers intent on preserving the country's cultural heritage when those who should have borne that task were abed. Such an array of the outrageous had not been seen since Genghis Khan swept down from the steppes, though that Lord of the Mongols had baulked at stretching as far as invading Glasgow because of the inherent danger in tangling with real barbarians.

"What did he mean, milk bottles?" Midden turned to ask Hugh who was on his pillion.

"Drop back, I'll ask him."

Midden throttled back and let Mixer, with Shame on the pillion of his Harley, catch up with him. "What's she up to, Shame?" Hugh roared.

The noise of the motorbike engines did not allow for lengthy explanation. "Petrol!" the Shame roared back.

Midden heard it and twisted his throttle to shoot forward again, nearly leaving Hugh sprawled in the street.

"Petrol, the bitch."

"Get to a phone, call the fire brigade."

"It's a firing squad I want for that sister of yours."

"It's the lack of sex, Hugh. She gets cranky when she's not getting laid."

"You said you would get her hitched up."

"Not one of my brave boys would take her on. Offered them money and everything."

They swept along the Expressway and worried messages flew over the police airwaves that the bikers were on a run and wondered what mayhem was about to ensue.

"This is crap," Hugh shouted to Midden, "Could you boys not get up to date and get helicopters."

"We're bypassing all that old technology," Midden replied, "We're going straight to jetpacks and Buck Rogers is joining next week."

"I'm not painting his tank," commented Hugh, who'd always been more of a Flash Gordon man.

17. THE STORMER REVEALED

Fiona had all her bottles lined up before her, their mouths stuffed with rags. She lifted one, felt the weight of it, then took the lighter she'd found in her glove box and set the rag on fire.

Crawford and his army marched into view with two policemen trailing behind them. Fiona, about to throw the petrol bomb at The Stormer, paused to see who was arriving.

Crawford led his troops to within yards of Fiona.

"Sod off, she's mine!" Fiona screamed.

Crawford's face was flushed. "We're with you, sister, burn the witch!"

Fiona glared at the intruders but tossed the bomb only to see it fall short and set a bench alight. Sirens grew louder as they approached.

Crawford and his old ladies moved in to help Fiona light her bombs.

Flashing blue lights announced the arrival of a police car and a fire engine.

An old woman tried throwing a bomb, but didn't have the strength to chuck it even a couple of yards. The old women scattered away from the flames.

The firemen tried to unravel hoses but the old ladies, excited by uniforms, threw themselves at them with a passion that was more than sexual.

Now Fiona hurled a bomb and it struck the wall, but too far away from the mural, and flames shot up from it.

Davina and Audrey pulled up in the car. Davina ran from the car and tried to stop Crawford throwing a bomb but she was held by a policeman.

More police cars arrived, sirens blaring and lights flashing.

A thunderous roar announced the arrival of Midden, Hugh and the bikers. They pulled up across from Davina, dismounted and watched the circus.

"What the hell's going on, Hugh?"

"Buggered if I know."

"Who's fighting who, because I'm not sending the boys into battle without some clearly defined objectives. I'm not an American president."

Hugh considered. "Fiona's out to do damage to the picture with her firebombs. Crawford there's trying to help her. The polis are just trying to keep the peace and the firemen are standing by in case Fiona manages to ever hit anything with a milk bottle."

"And the old women?"

"Fuck knows. Night out from the Women's Institute maybe."

"Gives a whole different meaning to grab a granny night."

A policewoman was struggling with Fiona. Old women were kicking firemen on the shin. Crawford had climbed onto a bench and was waving a blazing Molotov cocktail in the air.

With one hand he pointed an accusing finger at Davina.

"She's here!" he screeched. "The source of all temptation! Painted Jezebel! Whore of Babylon!"

Midden tried to stop him but Hugh pulled away and raced across the grass to dive at Crawford, catching him round the knees and sending him sprawling. It was worthy of Murrayfield and brought a cheer from the bikers. Crawford's petrol bomb rolled away and Hugh and Crawford punched ineffectually at each other. It was a clash of conflicting pains, Crawford's caused by the painting and Hugh's by the beating.

The police moved in to separate them and the bikers moved in to protect Hugh. It wasn't a real fight, mostly pushing and shoving, but as the policemen backed off they got scared and drew their batons and pepper sprays. Now the bikers backed off to their bikes. Audrey joined them and found a protector in Midden who urged her behind the phalanx of motorcycles.

Crawford saw his opportunity and ran off to pick up the bomb he'd dropped. He climbed on to the bench again and threw the bomb.

It arced through the inky sky and struck The Stormer full in the face. The petrol flooded over the mural and The Stormer was alight.

The pandemonium ceased, there was silence. Everybody watched The Stormer burn. For ages, even as the paint blistered and bubbled, her image remained and even smiled the smile of one who has achieved her aim. She had done her job, she had brought the crisis. A struggling Hugh was held by the bikers, tears streaming down his face.

Davina pulled away from the cop who was holding her.

"Hugh!" she shouted. "Time's up, Coop! Destiny's calling! Middle class housewife? Not wild enough?"

Hugh had a wild premonition of what was coming and shook his head wildly, held up his hands, signalling for her to stop.

"I am The Stormer!" she screamed.

It echoed back from the wall like shrill thunder. She started running towards Hugh, and as she ran she started shedding her clothes, every item seemingly designed to fall from her body. Her jacket went. Her blouse. Her bra. Her breasts bounced firmly in the cold air. Somehow she managed to shrug her jeans off while running. Her pants followed and she was as bare as The Stormer.

151

She streaked across the grass, naked now, her mane of red hair flying out behind her, lit by the burning Stormer. As she loped she was Diana, Goddess of the hunt, uncaring and intent on her prey.

Crawford remained standing on the bench, his jaw hanging. Everybody stopped and there was an even deeper silence, broken only by the crackle of flames. She was that thing they call poetry in motion and old, withered, women and hard-bitten, filthy bikers, seeing Davina McLean, The Stormer, being born, would remember this day for the rest of their lives.
Suddenly everybody came alive again and the cops tried to catch Davina. She remembered Hugh, the little dancing master, and dropped one hip, sending them all the wrong way. She shimmied, she shook, and laughed at the fact that this gave her an unfair advantage, for even policewomen could not help but gape at beauty personified. Soon, she was too far ahead for them, and came to a stop facing Hugh.
He nodded slowly and embraced her.
The bikers formed a barrier around them, and as the police approached they grabbed their own weapons, in the shape of bike chains and spanners from their bikes. Now it was the police who backed off.
Hugh removed his coat and covered Davina with it.
He climbed onto Midden's bike and she sat on the pillion, side-saddle. She was wrapped in his coat, her red hair billowing in the night wind. She put her arms round Hugh. He gunned the bike and they roared off.
Behind them, The Stormer burned.

Oh Glasgow.

Printed in the United Kingdom
by Lightning Source UK Ltd.
135291UK00002B/28-30/P